ONCE
UPON
A TIME

ONCE
UPON
A TIME

A COLLECTION OF
CLASSIC FAIRY TALES

ILLUSTRATED BY **KEVIN TONG**

HYPERION
NEW YORK

Collection copyright © 2012 Hyperion
Introduction copyright © 2012 ABC
Illustrations copyright © 2012 Hyperion
Once Upon a Time copyright © 2011 ABC Studios. All Rights Reserved.

Library of Congress Cataloging-in-Publication Data

Kinder- und Hausmärchen. English.
   Once upon a time : tales by the Brothers Grimm / illustrated by Kevin Tong.
     p. cm.
   ISBN 978-1-4013-2463-6
1. Fairy tales—Germany. I. Grimm, Jacob, 1785-1863. II. Grimm, Wilhelm, 1786-1859. III. Tong, Kevin, ill. IV. Title.
   GR166..K5313 2011
   398.20943—dc23
      2011036526

Hyperion books are available for special promotions and premiums. For details contact the HarperCollins Special Markets Department in the New York office at 212-207-7528, fax 212-207-7222, or email spsales@harpercollins.com.

BOOK DESIGN BY SHUBHANI SARKAR

FIRST EDITION

10 9 8 7 6 5 4

SUSTAINABLE FORESTRY INITIATIVE | Certified Sourcing
www.sfiprogram.org
SFI-00993

THIS LABEL APPLIES TO TEXT STOCK

We try to produce the most beautiful books possible, and we are also extremely concerned about the impact of our manufacturing process on the forests of the world and the environment as a whole. Accordingly, we've made sure that all of the paper we use has been certified as coming from forests that are managed, to ensure the protection of the people and wildlife dependent upon them.

CONTENTS

FOREWORD

Surely the Brothers Grimm could not have predicted the tremendous influence their collection of tales would have on literature. Yet, nearly two hundred years after the publication of the first volume of *Grimm's Fairy Tales*, the stories have become so integral to the fabric of our culture that we would hardly believe anyone who claimed not to know at least one of them. Perhaps our parents told us the tale of Little Red Riding Hood, maybe we read the story of Rumpelstiltskin in school, or it's possible we saw Disney's versions of *Snow White and the Seven Dwarfs* or *Cinderella*. However we encountered these magical tales, they are often among the first that we can remember learning and have become ubiquitous in our shared imagination.

The fact that these archetypal tales have persisted for so long in our minds as the foundation for storytelling became the inspiration for *Once Upon a Time*. Nine years ago, after finishing our work on the final season of *Felicity*, we sat down to discuss what type of show we would like to create. This led to a discussion of why we feel so compelled to tell stories. It didn't take us long to realize that the seed of this impulse was planted early in our childhoods when we first fell in love with these fairy tales and their characters. But while we knew we adored them all as they were, we also wished to learn more about what made them tick and the world they inhabited. This was a daunting task, and it wasn't until after our experience writing for *Lost*—where we continually balanced intricately constructed mythology with even more intricately constructed characters—that we felt ready to tackle this idea. The approach we took was to dig into the world of these iconic figures and find what it was about them that touched us so deeply. What we discovered was a powerful force that seemed to connect all these tales. Hope.

For us, that's what a fairy tale is. It's the ability to hope that your life will improve. It's the same reason we believe people buy lottery tickets—if you win, you get to quit your job and move to Paris. Or pursue whatever dream eludes you in your daily grind. These days, hope is especially important and relevant to our lives. We wanted to write something that, for one hour each week, could transport our audience to a place where they could set everything aside and remember the hope they felt as children reading these tales for the first time. That feeling of hope—that one can transcend the circumstances into which he or she was born, or that one can find, no matter how difficult it seems, true love—was the idea we wanted to build upon, and thus, *Grimm's Fairy Tales* became a jumping-off point for our show. The cherished place they hold in our hearts is what led us to delve into these characters and explore the icons we grew up with.

So with that in mind, it is an honor to introduce these classic tales in this new collection. The contemporary take we're attempting to bring to audiences week to week is marvelously reflected in the pages of this book through the artwork of Kevin Tong. His aesthetic seamlessly incorporates a thoroughly contemporary sensibility into an appreciation and mastery of classical styles. That is exactly what we hope to do with *Once Upon a Time*: to start with something we all know and love, and then turn it over, examine it from different perspectives, and make it new and exciting again. Like us, Kevin is clearly interested in discovering the unseen behind the seen, while at the same time always keeping sight of what it was that he found so fascinating about his subject matter in the first place.

We hope that this book, as well as our show, will encourage families and friends to find each other, to come together, and to share. We feel nostalgia for the time when we first read these tales as children, and we hope that this edition will provide an opportunity for adult readers to once again encounter the experience of their youth. Perhaps this book will even encourage some readers to share these timeless classics with their own children. Whatever purpose they serve, these stories will continue to endure in our collective consciousness; they will be printed and reprinted, and they will continue to inspire excitement and creativity long after our show has gone off the air. That fact, in and of itself, is truly hopeful.

EDWARD KITSIS & ADAM HOROWITZ

LOS ANGELES, 2011

ONCE
UPON
A TIME

HANSEL AND GRETHEL

Near a great forest there lived a poor woodcutter and his wife, and his two children. The boy's name was Hansel and the girl's Grethel. They had very little to bite or to sup, and once, when there was great dearth in the land, the man could not even gain the daily bread. As he lay in bed one night thinking of this, and turning and tossing, he sighed heavily, and said to his wife,

"What will become of us? We cannot even feed our children. There is nothing left for us."

"I will tell you what, husband," answered the wife. "We will take the children into the forest early in the morning, where it is thickest. We will make them a fire, and we will give each of them a piece of bread. Then we will go to our work and leave them alone. They will never find the way home again, and we shall be rid of them."

"No, wife," said the man. "I cannot do that. I cannot find it in my heart to take my children into the forest and to leave them there alone. The wild animals would soon come and devour them."

"Oh you fool," said she. "Then we will all four starve. You had better get the coffins ready." And she left him no peace until he consented.

"But I really pity the poor children," said the man.

The two children had not been able to sleep for hunger, and had heard what their stepmother had said to their father.

Grethel wept bitterly, and said to Hansel, "It is all over for us."

"Do be quiet, Grethel," said Hansel. "And do not fret. I will manage something." And when the parents had gone to sleep he got up, put on his little coat, opened the back door, and slipped out. The moon was shining brightly, and the white flints that lay in front of the house glistened like pieces of silver. Hansel stooped and filled the little pocket of his coat as full as it would hold.

Then he went back again, and said to Grethel, "Be easy, dear little sister, and go to sleep quietly. God will not forsake us," and laid himself down again in his bed.

When the day was breaking, and before the sun had risen, the wife came and awakened the two children.

"Get up, you lazy bones. We are going into the forest to cut wood," she said.

Then she gave each of them a piece of bread.

"That is for dinner," she told them, "and you must not eat it before then, for you will get no more."

Grethel carried the bread under her apron, for Hansel had his pockets full of the flints. Then they set off all together on their way to the forest. When they had gone a little way Hansel stood still and looked back towards the house, and this he did again and again.

Finally, his father said to him, "Hansel, what are you looking at? Take care not to forget your legs."

"O father," said Hansel, "I am looking at my little white kitten, who is sitting up on the roof to bid me good-bye."

"You young fool," said the woman, "that is not your kitten, but the sunshine on the chimney-pot."

Of course Hansel had not been looking at his kitten, but had been taking every now and then a flint from his pocket and dropping it on the road.

When they reached the middle of the forest the father told the children to collect wood to make a fire to keep them warm. Hansel and Grethel gathered enough brushwood for a little mountain and it was set on fire.

When the flame was burning quite high the wife said, "Now lie down by the fire and rest yourselves, you children, and we will go and cut wood. When we are ready, we will come and fetch you."

So Hansel and Grethel sat by the fire, and at noon they each ate their pieces of bread. They thought their father was in the wood all the time, as they seemed to hear the strokes of the axe, but really it was only a dry branch hanging to a withered tree that the wind moved to and fro. So when they had stayed there a long time their eyelids closed with weariness, and they fell fast asleep. When at last they woke it was night, and Grethel began to cry, and said,

"How shall we ever get out of this wood?" But Hansel comforted her, saying,

"Wait a little while longer, until the moon rises, and then we can easily find the way home."

And when the full moon got up, Hansel took his little sister by the hand and followed the way where the flint stones shone like silver and showed them the road. They walked on the whole night through, and at the break of day they came to their father's house. They knocked at the door, and when the wife opened it and saw that it was Hansel and Grethel she said,

"You naughty children, why did you sleep so long in the wood? We thought you were never coming home again!"

But the father was glad, for it had gone to his heart to leave them both in the woods alone.

Not very long after that there was again great scarcity in those parts, and the children heard their mother say at night in bed to their father,

"Everything is finished up. We have only half a loaf, and after that the tale comes to an end. The children must be off.

We will take them farther into the wood this time, so that they shall not be able to find the way back again. There is no other way to manage."

The man felt sad at heart, and he thought,

"It would better to share one's last morsel with one's children."

But the wife would listen to nothing that he said, but scolded and reproached him. He who says A must say B too, and when a man has given in once he has to do it a second time.

But the children were not asleep, and had heard all the talk. When the parents had gone to sleep Hansel got up to go out and get more flint stones as he had done before, but the wife had locked the door, and Hansel could not get out. He comforted his little sister, and said,

"Don't cry, Grethel, and go to sleep quietly, and God will help us."

Early the next morning the wife came and pulled the children out of bed. She gave them each a little piece of bread—less than before—and on the way to the wood Hansel crumbled the bread in his pocket, and often stopped to throw a crumb on the ground.

"Hansel, what are you stopping behind and staring for?" said the father.

"I am looking at my little pigeon sitting on the roof, to say good-bye to me," answered Hansel.

"You fool," said the wife, "that is no pigeon, but the morning sun shining on the chimney pots."

Hansel went on as before, and strewed bread crumbs all along the road.

The woman led the children far into the wood, where they had never been before in all their lives. And again there was a large fire made, and the mother said,

"Sit still there, you children, and when you are tired you can go to sleep. We are going into the forest to cut wood, and in the evening, when we are ready to go home we will come and fetch you."

So when noon came Grethel shared her bread with Hansel, who had strewn his along the road. Then they went to sleep, and the evening passed, and no one came for the poor children. When they awoke it was dark night, and Hansel comforted his little sister, and said,

"Wait a little, Grethel, until the moon gets up, then we shall be able to see the way home by the crumbs of bread that I have scattered along it."

So when the moon rose they got up, but they could find no crumbs of bread, for the birds of the woods and of the fields had come and picked them up. Hansel thought they might find the way all the same, but they could not. They went on all that night, and the next day from the morning until the evening, but they could not find the way out of the wood, and they were very hungry, for they had nothing to eat but the few berries they could pick up. And when they were so tired that they could no longer drag themselves along, they lay down under a tree and fell asleep.

It was now the third morning since they had left their father's house. They were always trying to get back to it, but instead only found themselves farther in the wood, and if help had not soon come they would have been starved. About noon they saw a pretty snow-white bird sitting on a bough, and singing so sweetly that they stopped to listen. And when he had finished the bird spread his wings and flew before them, and they followed after him until they came to a little house, and the bird perched on the roof, and when they came nearer they saw that the house was built of bread and roofed with cakes, and the window was of transparent sugar.

"We will have some of this," said Hansel, "and make a fine meal. I will eat a piece of the roof, Grethel, and you can have some of the window—that will taste sweet."

So Hansel reached up and broke off a bit of the roof, just to see how it tasted, and Grethel stood by the window and gnawed at it. Then they heard a thin voice call out from inside,

"Nibble, nibble, like a mouse,
Who is nibbling at my house?"

And the children answered,

"Never mind,
It is the wind."

And they went on eating, never disturbing themselves. Hansel, who found that the roof tasted very nice, took down a great piece of it, and Grethel pulled out a large round windowpane, and sat down and began to eat it. Then the door opened, and an aged woman came out, leaning upon a crutch. Hansel and Grethel felt very frightened, and let fall what they had in their hands. The old woman, however, nodded her head, and said,

"Ah, my dear children, why are you here? You must come indoors and stay with me, you will be no trouble."

So she took them each by the hand and led them into her little house. And there they found a good meal of milk and pancakes, with sugar, apples, and nuts. After that, she showed them two little white beds, and Hansel and Grethel laid themselves down, and thought they were in heaven.

Although her behavior was so kind, the old woman was a wicked witch who lay in wait for children, and had built the little house on purpose to entice them. Once they were inside, she killed them, cooked them, and ate them. The witch's eyes were red, and she could not see very far, but she had a keen scent, like the beasts, and knew very well when human creatures were near. When she knew that Hansel and Grethel were coming, she gave a spiteful laugh, and said triumphantly,

"I have them, and they shall not escape me!"

Early in the morning, before the children were awake, she got up to look at them, and as they lay sleeping so peacefully with round rosy cheeks, she said to herself,

"What a fine feast I shall have!"

Then she grasped Hansel with her withered hand, and led him into a little stable, and shut him up behind a grating. Call and scream as he might, it was no good. Then she went back to Grethel and shook her, crying,

"Get up, lazy bones. Fetch water, and cook something nice for your brother. He is outside in the stable, and must be fattened up. And when he is fat enough I will eat him."

Grethel began to weep bitterly, but it was of no use. She had to do what the wicked witch bade her.

And so the best kind of victuals was cooked for poor Hansel, while Grethel got nothing but crab shells. Each morning the old woman visited the little stable, and cried,

"Hansel, stretch out your finger so that I may tell if you will soon be fat enough."

Hansel, however, used to hold out a little bone, and the old woman, who had weak eyes, could not see what it was, and supposing it to be Hansel's finger, wondered very much that it was not getting fatter. When four weeks had passed and Hansel seemed to remain so thin, she lost patience and could wait no longer.

"Now then, Grethel," she cried to the little girl, "be quick and draw water. Be Hansel fat or be he lean, tomorrow I must kill and cook him."

Oh what a grief for the poor little sister to have to fetch water, and how the tears flowed down over her cheeks!

"Dear God, pray help us!" cried she. "If we had been devoured by wild beasts in the wood, at least we should have died together."

"Spare me your lamentations," said the old woman. "They are of no use."

Early next morning, Grethel had to get up, make the fire, and fill the kettle.

"First we will do the baking," said the old woman. "I have heated the oven already, and kneaded the dough."

She pushed poor Grethel towards the oven, out of which the flames were already shining.

"Creep in," said the witch, "and see if it is properly hot, so that the bread may be baked."

Once Grethel climbed in, the witch intended to shut the door upon the girl and let her be baked, and then she would have eaten her. But Grethel perceived her intention, and said,

"I don't know how to do it. How shall I get in?"

"Stupid goose," said the old woman. "The opening is big enough, do you see? I could get in myself!" and she stooped down and put her head in the oven's mouth. Then Grethel gave her a push, so that she went in farther, and she shut the iron door upon her and put up the bar. Oh how frightfully she howled! But Grethel ran away, and left the wicked witch to burn miserably. Grethel went straight to Hansel, opened the stable-door, and cried,

"Hansel, we are free! The old witch is dead!"

Then out flew Hansel like a bird from its cage as soon as the door is opened. How happy they both were! How they fell each on the other's neck and danced about! And as they had nothing more to fear, they went all over the old witch's house, and in every corner there stood chests of pearls and precious stones.

"This is something better than flint stones," said Hansel, as he filled his pockets, and Grethel, thinking she also would like to carry something home with her, filled her apron full.

"Now, away we go, if we only can get out of the witch's wood," said Hansel.

When they had journeyed a few hours, they came to a great body of water.

"We can never get across this," said Hansel. "I see no stepping-stones and no bridge."

"And there is no boat either," said Grethel. "But here comes a white duck! If I ask her, she will help us over." So Grethel cried,

"Duck, duck, here we stand,
Hansel and Grethel, on the land,
Stepping-stones and bridge we lack,
Carry us over on your nice white back."

And the duck came accordingly, and Hansel got upon her and told his sister to come too.

"No," answered Grethel, "that would be too hard upon the duck. We can go separately, one after the other."

And that was how it was managed, and after that they went on happily, until they came to the wood, and the way grew more and more familiar, until at last they saw in the distance their father's house. Then they ran until they came upon it, rushed in the door, and fell on their father's neck. The man had not had a quiet hour since he left his children in the wood, but the wife had died. And when Grethel opened her apron, the pearls and precious stones were scattered all over the room, and Hansel took one handful after another out of his pocket. Then was all care at an end, and they lived in great joy together.

SIX SOLDIERS OF FORTUNE

There was once a man who was a jack-of-all-trades. He had served in the war, and had been brave and bold, but at the end of it he was sent about his business with three farthings and his discharge.

"I am not going to stand this," said he. "Wait until I find the right man to help me, and the King shall give me all the treasures of his kingdom before he has done with me."

Then, full of wrath, he went into the forest, and he saw a man standing by six trees which he had rooted up as if they had been stalks of corn. And he said to him,

"Will you be my man, and come along with me?"

"All right," answered he. "I must just take this bit of wood home to my father and mother." And taking one of the trees, he bound it round the other five, and putting the bundle on his shoulder, carried it off. Then soon coming back, he went along with his leader, who said,

"Two such as we can stand against the whole world."

And when they had gone on a little while, they came to a

huntsman who was kneeling on one knee and taking careful aim with his rifle.

"Huntsman," said the leader, "what are you aiming at?"

"Two miles from here," answered he, "there sits a fly on the bough of an oak-tree. I mean to put a bullet into its left eye."

"Oh, come along with me," said the leader. "Three of us together can stand against the world."

The huntsman was quite willing to go with him, and so they went on until they came to seven windmills whose sails were going round briskly, and yet there was no wind blowing from any quarter, and not a leaf stirred.

"Well," said the leader, "I cannot think what ails the windmills, turning without wind." And he went on with his followers about two miles farther, and then they came to a man sitting up in a tree, holding one nostril and blowing with the other.

"Now then," said the leader, "what are you doing up there?"

"Two miles from here," answered he, "there are seven windmills. I am blowing, and they are going round."

"Oh, go with me," cried the leader. "Four of us together can stand against the world."

So the blower got down and went with them, and after a time they came to a man standing on one leg, and the other had been taken off and was lying near him.

"You seem to have got a handy way of resting yourself," said the leader to the man.

"I am a runner," answered he, "and in order to keep myself from going too fast I have taken off a leg, for when I run with both, I go faster than a bird can fly."

"Oh, go with me," cried the leader. "Five of us together may well stand against the world."

So he went with them all together, and it was not long before they met a man with a little hat on, and he wore it just over one ear.

"Manners! Manners!" said the leader. "With your hat like that, you look like a jack-fool."

"I dare not put it straight," answered the other. "If I did, there would be such a terrible frost that the very birds would be frozen and fall dead from the sky to the ground."

"Oh, come with me," said the leader. "We six together may well stand against the whole world."

So the six went on until they came to a town where the King had caused it to be made known that whoever would run a race with his daughter and win it might become her husband, but that whoever lost must lose his head in the bargain. And the leader came forward and said one of his men should run for him.

"Then," said the King, "his life too must be put in pledge, and if he fails, his head and yours too must fall."

When this was quite settled and agreed upon, the leader called the runner and strapped his second leg on to him.

"Now, look out," said he, "and take care that we win."

It had been agreed that the one who should bring water first from a far distant brook should be accounted winner. Now the King's daughter and the runner each took a pitcher, and they started both at the same time. But in one moment, when the King's daughter had gone but a very little way, the runner was out of sight, for his running was as if the wind rushed by. In a short time he reached the brook, filled his pitcher full of water, and turned back again. About halfway home, however, he was overcome with weariness. He set down his pitcher and lay down on the ground to sleep. But in order to awaken soon again by not lying too soft, he had taken a horse's skull which lay near and placed it under his head for a pillow. In the meanwhile the King's daughter, who really was a good runner—good enough to beat an ordinary man—had reached the brook and filled her pitcher, and was hastening with it back again when she saw the runner lying asleep.

"The day is mine," said she with much joy, and she emptied his pitcher and hastened on. And now all had been lost but for the huntsman who was standing on the castle wall, and with his keen eyes saw all that happened.

"We must not be outdone by the King's daughter," said he, and he loaded his rifle and took so good an aim that he shot the horse's skull from under the runner's head without doing him any harm. And the runner awoke and jumped up, and saw his pitcher standing empty and the King's daughter far on her way home. But, not losing courage, he ran swiftly to the brook, filled it again with water, and for all that, he got home ten minutes before the King's daughter.

"Look you," said he. "This is the first time I have really stretched my legs. Before it was not worth the name of running."

The King was vexed, and his daughter yet more so, that she should be beaten by a discharged common soldier. And they took counsel together how they might rid themselves of him and of his companions at the same time.

"I have a plan," said the King. "Do not fear but that we shall be quit of them forever." Then he went out to the men and bade them to feast and be merry and eat and drink. And he led them into a room with a floor of iron, and the doors were iron, the windows had iron frames and bolts. In the room was a table set out with costly food.

"Now, go in there and make yourselves comfortable," said the King.

And when they had gone in, he had the door locked and bolted. Then he called the cook, and told him to make a big fire underneath the room, so that the iron floor of it should be red hot. And the cook did so, and the six men began to feel the room growing very warm, by reason, as they thought at first, of the good dinner. But as the heat grew greater and greater, and they found the doors and windows fastened, they began to think it was an evil plan of the King's to suffocate them.

"He shall not succeed, however," said the man with the little hat. "I will bring on a frost that shall make the fire feel ashamed of itself, and creep out of the way."

So he set his hat straight on his head, and immediately there came such a frost that all the heat passed away and the food froze in the dishes. After an hour or two had passed, and the King thought they must have all perished in the heat, he opened the door and went to see how they fared. And when the door flew back, there they were all six quite safe and sound, and they said they were quite ready to come out, so that they might warm themselves, for the great cold of that room had caused the food to freeze in the dishes. Full of wrath, the King went to the cook and scolded him, and asked why he had not done as he was ordered.

"It is hot enough there. You may see for yourself," answered the cook. And the King looked and saw an immense fire burning underneath the room of iron, and he began to think that the six men were not to be got rid of in that way. And he thought of a new plan by which it might be managed, so he sent for the leader and said to him,

"If you will give up your right to my daughter, and take gold instead, you may have as much as you like."

"Certainly, my lord King," answered the man. "Let me have as much gold as my servant can carry, and I give up all claim to your daughter." And the King agreed that he should come again in a fortnight to fetch the gold. The man then called together all the tailors in the kingdom, and set them to work to make a sack, and it took them a fortnight. And when it was ready, the strong man who had been found rooting up trees took it on his shoulder, and went to the King.

"Who is this immense fellow carrying on his shoulder a bundle of stuff as big as a house?" cried the King, terrified to think how much gold he would carry off. And a ton of gold was dragged in by sixteen strong men, but he put it all into the sack with one hand, saying,

"Why don't you bring some more? This hardly covers the bottom!" So the King bade them fetch by degrees the whole of his treasure, and even then the sack was not half full.

"Bring more!" cried the man. "These few scraps go no way at all!" Then at last seven thousand wagons laden with gold collected through the whole kingdom were driven up and he threw them in his sack, oxen and all.

"I will not look too closely," said he, "but take what I can get, so long as the sack is full." And when all was put in there was still plenty of room.

"I must make an end of this," he said. "If it is not full, it is so much the easier to tie up." And he hoisted it on his back, and went off with his comrades.

When the King saw all the wealth of his realm carried off by a single man he was full of wrath, and he bade his cavalry mount their horses, follow after the six men, and take the sack away from the strong man.

Two regiments were soon up to them, and called them to consider themselves prisoners and to deliver up the sack, or be cut in pieces.

"Prisoners, say you?" said the man who could blow. "Suppose you first have a little dance together in the air," and holding one nostril, and blowing through the other, he sent the regiments flying head over heels, over the hills and far away. But a sergeant who had nine wounds and was a brave fellow, begged not to be put to so much shame. And the blower let him down easily, so that he came to no harm, and he bade him go to the King and tell him that whatever regiments he liked to send more should be blown away just the same. And the King, when he got the message, said,

"Let the fellows be. They have some right on their side." So the six comrades carried home their treasure, divided it among them, and lived contented until they died.

CAT AND MOUSE
IN PARTNERSHIP

A cat, having made acquaintance with a mouse, professed such great love and friendship for her, that the mouse at last agreed that they should live and keep house together.

"We must make provision for the winter," said the cat, "or we shall suffer hunger, and you, little mouse, must not stir out, or you will be caught in a trap."

So they took counsel together and bought a little pot of fat. But they could not tell where to put it for safety. Finally, after long consideration, the cat said there could not be a better place than the church, for nobody would steal there. And they would put it under the altar and not touch it until they were really in want. So this was done, and the little pot placed in safety.

But before long the cat was seized with a great wish to taste it.

"Listen to me, little mouse," said he. "I have been asked by my cousin to be the godfather to a little son she has brought into the world. He is white with brown spots and they want to have the christening today, so let me go to it, and you stay at home and keep house."

"Oh yes, certainly," answered the mouse. "Pray go by all means. And when you are feasting on all the good things, think of me. I should so like a drop of the sweet red wine."

But there was not a word of truth in all this. The cat had no cousin, and had not been asked to stand godfather. Rather, he went to the church, straight up to the little pot, and licked the fat off the top. Then he took a walk over the roofs of the town, saw his acquaintances, stretched himself in the sun, and licked his whiskers as often as he thought of the little pot of fat. And then when it was evening he went home.

"Here you are at last," said the mouse. "I expect you have had a merry time."

"Oh, pretty well," answered the cat.

"And what name did you give the child?" asked the mouse.

"Top-off," answered the cat, drily.

"Top-off!" cried the mouse. "That is a singular and wonderful name! Is it common in your family?"

"What does it matter?" said the cat. "It's not any worse than Crumb-picker, like your godchild."

A little time after this the cat was again seized with a longing.

"Again I must ask you," said he to the mouse, "to do me a

favor, and keep house alone for a day. I have been asked a second time to stand godfather. And as the little one has a white ring round its neck, I cannot well refuse."

So the kind little mouse consented, and the cat crept along by the town wall until he reached the church, and going straight to the little pot of fat, devoured half of it.

"Nothing tastes so well as what one keeps to oneself," said he, feeling quite content with his day's work. When he reached home, the mouse asked what name had been given to the child.

"Half-gone," answered the cat.

"Half-gone!" cried the mouse. "I never heard such a name in my life!"

Soon after that the cat's mouth began to water again for the fat.

"Good things always come in threes," said he to the mouse. "Again I have been asked to stand godfather. The little one is quite black with white feet, and not any white hair on its body. Such a thing does not happen every day, so you will let me go, won't you?"

"Top-off, Half-gone," murmured the mouse. "They are such curious names, I cannot but wonder at them!"

"That's because you are always sitting at home," said the cat, "in your little gray frock and hairy tail, never seeing the world, and fancying all sorts of things."

So the little mouse cleaned up the house and set it all in

order. Meanwhile the greedy cat went and made an end of the little pot of fat.

"Now that all is finished one's mind will be easy," said he, and came home in the evening, quite sleek and comfortable. The mouse asked at once what name had been given to the third child.

"It won't please you any better than the others," answered the cat. "It is called All-gone."

"All-gone!" cried the mouse. "What an unheard-of name! I never heard of anything like it! All-gone! Whatever can it mean?" And shaking her head, she curled herself round and went to sleep. After that, the cat did not again ask to stand godfather.

When the winter had come and there was nothing more to be had outdoors, the mouse began to think of their store in the church.

"Come, cat," said she. "We will fetch our pot of fat. How good it will taste, to be sure!"

"Of course it will," said the cat. "Just as good as if you stuck your tongue out of a window!"

So they set out, and when they reached the place, they found the pot, but it was standing empty.

"Oh! Now I know what it all meant," cried the mouse. "Now I see what sort of a partner you have been! Instead of standing godfather you have devoured it all up. First Top-off, then Half-gone, then—"

"Will you hold your tongue!" screamed the cat. "Another word and I devour you too!"

And the poor little mouse, already having "All-gone" on her tongue, let it slip out, and the cat leapt upon her and made an end of her. And that is the way of the world.

CINDERELLA

There was once a rich man whose wife lay sick, and when she felt her end drawing near she called to her only daughter to come near her bed, and said,

"Dear child, be pious and good, and God will always take care of you, and I will look down upon you from heaven, and will be with you."

And then she closed her eyes and expired. The maiden went every day to her mother's grave and wept, and was always pious and good. When the winter came the snow covered the grave with a white covering, and when the sun came in the early spring and melted it away, the man took another wife.

The new wife brought two daughters home with her, and they were beautiful and fair in appearance, but at heart were black and ugly. And then began very evil times for the poor stepdaughter.

They took away her pretty dresses and put on her an old gray apron, and gave her wooden shoes to wear.

"Just look now at the proud princess, how she is decked

out!" they cried, laughing, and sent her into the kitchen. There she was obliged to do heavy work from morning to night, get up early in the morning, draw water, make the fires, cook, and wash. Besides that, the sisters did their utmost to torment her. They mocked her, and strew peas and lentils among the ashes, and set her to pick them up. In the evenings, when she was quite tired out with her hard day's work, she had no bed to lie on but was obliged to rest on the hearth among the cinders. And as she always looked dusty and dirty, they named her Cinderella.

It happened one day that the father went to the fair, and he asked his two stepdaughters what he should bring back for them.

"Fine clothes!" said one.

"Pearls and jewels!" said the other.

"But what will you have, Cinderella?" said he.

"The first twig that strikes against your hat on the way home. That is what I should like you to bring me."

So he bought for the two stepdaughters fine clothes, pearls, and jewels, and on his way back, as he rode through a green lane, a twig from a hazel tree struck against his hat. He broke it off and carried it home with him. And when he reached home he gave to the stepdaughters what they had wished for, and to Cinderella he gave the twig. She thanked him, and went to her mother's grave, and planted this twig there, weeping so bitterly that the tears fell upon it and watered it, and it flourished and became a fine hazel tree. Cinderella went to see it three times a day, and wept and prayed. Each time a white bird rose up from the tree, and if she uttered any wish the bird brought her whatever she had wished for.

Now it came to pass that the King ordained a festival that should last for three days, and to which all the beautiful young women of that country were invited so that the King's son might choose a bride from among them. When the two stepdaughters heard that they too were invited to appear, they felt very pleased and they called Cinderella, and said,

"Comb our hair, brush our shoes, and make our buckles fast, we are going to the wedding feast at the King's castle."

When she heard this, Cinderella could not help crying for she too would have liked to go to the dance, and she begged her stepmother to allow her.

"What, you, Cinderella?" said she. "In all your dust and dirt, you want to go to the festival! You that have no dress and no shoes! You want to dance!"

But as she persisted in asking, at last the stepmother said,

"I have strewed a dish of lentils in the ashes, and if you can pick them all up again in two hours, you may go with us."

Then the maiden went to the back door that led into the garden, and called out,

"O gentle doves, O turtledoves,
And all the birds that be,
The lentils that in ashes lie

Come and pick up for me!
The good must be put in the dish,
The bad you may eat if you wish."

Then there came to the kitchen window two white doves, and after them some turtledoves, and at last a crowd of all the birds under heaven, chirping and fluttering, and they landed among the ashes. The doves nodded with their heads and began to pick, peck, pick, peck, and then all the others began to pick, peck, pick, peck, and put all the good grains into the dish. Before an hour was over all was done, and they flew away. Then the maiden brought the dish to her stepmother, feeling joyful and thinking that now she should go to the feast. But the stepmother said,

"No, Cinderella, you have no proper clothes, and you do not know how to dance, and you would be laughed at!"

And when Cinderella cried for disappointment, she added,

"If you can pick two dishes full of lentils out of the ashes, nice and clean, you shall go with us," thinking to herself, "for that is not possible." When she had strewn two dishes full of lentils among the ashes the maiden went through the back door into the garden, and cried,

"O gentle doves, O turtledoves,
And all the birds that be,
The lentils that in ashes lie

Come and pick up for me!
The good must be put in the dish,
The bad you may eat if you wish."

So there came to the kitchen window two white doves, and then some turtledoves, and at last a crowd of all the other birds under heaven, chirping and fluttering, and they alighted among the ashes, and the doves nodded with their heads and began to pick, peck, pick, peck, and then all the others began to pick, peck, pick, peck, and put all the good grains into the dish. And before half an hour was over it was all done, and they flew away. Then the maiden took the dishes to the stepmother, feeling joyful, and thinking that now she should go with them to the feast. But she said, "All this is of no good to you. You cannot come with us, for you have no proper clothes, and cannot dance. You would put us to shame."

Then she turned her back on poor Cinderella, and made haste to set out with her two proud daughters.

And as there was no one left in the house, Cinderella went to her mother's grave, under the bush, and cried,

"Little tree, little tree, shake over me,
That silver and gold may come down and cover me."

Then the bird threw down a dress of gold and silver, and a pair of slippers embroidered with silk and silver. And in all haste she put on the dress and went to the festival. But her stepmother and sisters did not know her, and she looked so beautiful in her golden dress that they thought she must be a foreign princess. Of Cinderella they never thought at all, and supposed that she was sitting at home picking the lentils out of the ashes. The King's son came to meet her, and took her by the hand and danced with her, and he refused to stand up with anyone else, so that he might not be obliged to let her hand go. And when anyone came to claim it he answered,

"She is my partner."

And when the sunset came she wanted to go home, but the prince said he would go with her to take care of her, for he wanted to see where the beautiful maiden lived. But she escaped him as they neared her house and jumped up into the bird house. Then the prince waited until her father came, and told him the strange maiden had jumped into the bird house. The father thought to himself,

"It cannot surely be Cinderella," and called for axes and hatchets, and had the bird house cut down, but there was no one in it. And when they entered the house there sat Cinderella in her dirty clothes among the cinders, and a little oil lamp burnt dimly in the chimney. For Cinderella had been very quick, and had jumped out of the bird house again, and had run to the hazel bush. And there she had taken off her beautiful dress and had laid it on the grave, and the bird had carried it away again, and then she had put on her little gray apron again, and had sat down in the kitchen among the cinders.

The next day, when the festival began anew, and the parents and stepsisters had gone to it, Cinderella went to the hazel bush and cried,

"Little tree, little tree, shake over me,
That silver and gold may come down and cover me."

Then the bird cast down a still more splendid dress than on the day before. And when she appeared in it among the guests everyone was astonished at her beauty. The prince had been waiting until she came, and he took her hand and danced with her alone. And when anyone else came to invite her he said,

"She is my partner."

And when the sunset came she wanted to go home, and the prince followed her, for he wanted to see to what house she belonged. But she broke away from him, and ran into the garden at the back of the house. There stood a fine large tree, bearing splendid pears. She leapt as lightly as a squirrel among the branches, and the prince did not know what had become of her. So he waited until her father came, and then he told him that the strange maiden had rushed from him, and that he thought she had gone up into the pear tree. The father thought to himself,

"It cannot surely be Cinderella," and called for an axe, and felled the tree, but there was no one in it. And when they went into the kitchen there sat Cinderella among the cinders, as usual, for she had got down the other side of the tree, and had taken back her beautiful clothes to the bird on the hazel bush, and had put on her old gray kirtle again.

On the third day, when the parents and the stepsisters had set off, Cinderella went again to her mother's grave, and said to the tree,

"Little tree, little tree, shake over me,
That silver and gold may come down and cover me."

Then the bird cast down a dress the likes of which had never been seen for splendor and brilliancy, and slippers that were of gold.

And when she appeared in this dress at the feast, nobody knew what to say for wonderment. The prince danced with her alone, and if anyone else asked her he answered,

"She is my partner."

And when the sunset came, Cinderella wanted to go home and the prince was about to go with her, when she ran past him so quickly that he could not follow her. But he had laid a plan, and had caused all the steps to be spread with pitch, so that as she rushed down them the left shoe of the maiden remained sticking in it. The prince picked it up, and saw that it was of gold, and very small and slender. The next morning he went to her father and told him that none should be his bride save the one whose foot the golden shoe should fit. Then the two sisters were very glad, because they had pretty feet. The eldest went to her room to try on the shoe, and her mother stood by. But she could not get her great toe into it, for the shoe was too small. Then her mother handed her a knife, and said,

"Cut the toe off, for when you are Queen you will never have to go on foot." So the girl cut her toe off, squeezed her foot into the shoe, concealed the pain, and went down to the prince. Then he took her with him on his horse as his bride, and rode off. They had to pass by the grave, and there sat two pigeons on the hazel bush, and cried,

"There they go, there they go!
There is blood on her shoe.
The shoe is too small,
—Not the right bride at all!"

Then the prince looked at her shoe, and saw the blood flowing. And he turned his horse round and took the false bride home again, saying she was not the right one, and that the other sister must try on the shoe. So she went into her room to do so, and got her toes comfortably in, but her heel was too large. Then her mother handed her the knife, saying,

"Cut a piece off your heel. When you are Queen you will never have to go on foot."

So the girl cut a piece off her heel, and thrust her foot into the shoe, concealed the pain, and went down to the prince, who took his bride before him on his horse and rode off. When they passed by the hazel bush the two pigeons sat there and cried,

"There they go, there they go!
There is blood on her shoe.
The shoe is too small,
—Not the right bride at all!"

Then the prince looked at her foot, and saw how the blood was flowing from the shoe and staining the white stocking. And he turned his horse round and brought the false bride home again.

"This is not the right one," said he. "Have you no other daughter?"

"No," said the man. "Only my dead wife left behind her a little stunted Cinderella. It is impossible that she can be the bride." But the King's son ordered her to be sent for, but the mother said,

"Oh no! She is much too dirty. I could not let her be seen."

But he would have her fetched, and so Cinderella had to appear.

First she washed her face and hands quite clean, and went in and curtseyed to the prince, who held out to her the golden shoe. Then she sat down on a stool, drew her foot out of the heavy wooden shoe, and slipped it into the golden one, which fitted it perfectly. And when she stood up, and the prince looked in her face, he knew again the beautiful maiden that had danced with him, and he cried,

"This is the right bride!"

The stepmother and the two sisters were thunderstruck, and grew pale with anger. But he put Cinderella before him on his horse and rode off. And as they passed the hazel bush, the two white pigeons cried,

"There they go, there they go!
No blood on her shoe.
The shoe's not too small,
The right bride after all."

And when they had thus cried, they came flying after and perched on Cinderella's shoulders, one on the right, the other on the left, and so remained.

And when her wedding with the prince was appointed to be held the stepsisters came, hoping to find their way into Cinderella's good graces and to take part in the festivities. So as the bridal procession went to the church, the eldest walked on the right side and the younger on the left, and the pigeons picked out an eye of each of them. And as they returned the elder was on the left side and the younger on the right, and the pigeons picked out the other eye of each of them. And so they were condemned to go blind for the rest of their days because of their wickedness and falsehood.

THE THREE SPINSTERS

There was once a girl who was lazy and would not spin, and her mother could not persuade her to it, do what she would. At last the mother became angry and out of patience, and gave her a good beating, so that she cried out loudly. It happened that at that moment, the Queen was passing by. As she heard the crying, she stopped and, going into the house, asked the mother why she was beating her daughter, so that everyone outside in the street could hear her cries.

The woman was ashamed to tell of her daughter's laziness, so she said,

"I cannot stop her from spinning. She is forever at it, and I am poor and cannot furnish her with flax enough."

Then the Queen answered,

"I like nothing better than the sound of the spinning wheel, and always feel happy when I hear its humming. Let me take your daughter with me to the castle where I have plenty of flax. She shall spin there to her heart's content."

The mother was only too glad of the offer, and the Queen took the girl with her. When they reached the castle, the

Queen showed her three rooms which were filled with the finest flax as full as they could hold.

"Now you can spin me this flax," said she. "And when you can show me it is all done, you shall have my eldest son for husband. You may be poor, but I make nothing of that—your hard work is dowry enough."

The girl was inwardly terrified, for she could not have spun the flax even if she were to live to be one hundred years old and were to sit spinning every day of her life from morning to evening. And when she found herself alone she began to weep, and sat so for three days without beginning. On the third day the Queen came, and when she saw that nothing had been done of the spinning she was much surprised. But the girl excused herself by saying that she had not been able to begin because of the distress she was in at leaving her home and her mother. The excuse contented the Queen, who said, however, as she went away,

"Tomorrow you must begin to work."

When the girl found herself alone again she could not tell how to help herself or what to do, and in her perplexity she went and gazed out of the window. There she saw three women passing by. The first of them had a broad flat foot, the second had a big under-lip that hung down over her chin, and the third had a remarkably broad thumb. They all stopped in front of the window, and called out to know what it was that the girl wanted. She told them all her need and they promised her their help, and said,

"Then will you invite us to your wedding, and not be

ashamed of us, and call us your cousins, and let us sit at your table. If you will promise this, we will finish off your flax-spinning in a very short time."

"With all my heart," answered the girl. "Only come in now, and begin at once."

Then these same women came in, and she cleared a space in the first room for them to sit and carry on their spinning. The first one drew out the thread and moved the pedal that turned the wheel, the second moistened the thread, the third twisted it and rapped with her finger on the table, and as often as she rapped a heap of yarn fell to the ground, and it was most beautifully spun. But the girl hid the three spinsters out of the Queen's sight, and only showed her, as often as she came, the heaps of well-spun yarn. And there was no end to the praises she received. When the first room was empty they went on to the second, and then to the third, so that at last all was finished. Then the three women took their leave, saying to the girl,

"Do not forget what you have promised, and it will be all the better for you."

So when the girl took the Queen and showed her the empty rooms and the great heaps of yarn, the wedding was at once arranged, and the prince rejoiced that he should have so clever and diligent a wife, and praised her exceedingly.

"I have three cousins," said the girl. "As they have shown me a great deal of kindness, I would not wish to forget them in my good fortune. May I be allowed to invite them to the wedding, and to ask them to sit at the table with us?"

The Queen and the prince said at once,

"There is no reason against it."

So when the feast began in came the three spinsters in strange guise, and the bride said,

"Dear cousins, you are welcome."

"Oh," said the bridegroom. "Why do you have such dreadfully ugly relations?"

And then he went up to the first spinster and said,

"How is it that you have such a broad flat foot?"

"With treading," answered she. "With treading."

Then he went up to the second and said,

"How is it that you have such a great hanging lip?"

"With licking," answered she. "With licking."

Then he asked the third,

"How is it that you have such a broad thumb?"

"With twisting thread," answered she. "With twisting thread."

Then the prince said that from that time forward his beautiful bride should never touch a spinning wheel again, for he secretly feared she would one day look like her ugly cousins.

And so she escaped that tiresome flax-spinning.

THE GOLDEN GOOSE

There was a man who had three sons, the youngest of whom was called the Simpleton and was despised, laughed at, and neglected on every occasion. It happened one day that the eldest son wished to go into the forest to cut wood, and before he went his mother gave him a delicious pancake and a flask of wine, so that he might not suffer from hunger or thirst. When he came into the forest a little old gray man met him, who wished him good day, and said,

"Give me a bit of cake out of your pocket, and let me have a drink of your wine. I am so hungry and thirsty."

But the prudent youth answered,

"Give you my cake and my wine? I haven't got any. Be off with you."

And leaving the little man standing there, he went off. Then he began to fell a tree, but he had not been at it long before he made a wrong stroke, and the hatchet hit him in the arm, so that he was obliged to go home and get it bound up. That was what came of the little gray man.

Afterwards the second son went into the wood, and the mother gave to him, as to the eldest, a pancake and a flask of wine. The little old gray man met him also, and begged for a little bit of cake and a drink of wine. But the second son spoke out plainly, saying,

"What I give you I lose myself, so be off with you."

And leaving the little man standing there, he went off. The punishment followed. As he was chopping away at the tree, he hit himself in the leg so severely that he had to be carried home.

Then said the Simpleton,

"Father, let me go for once into the forest to cut wood." And the father answered, "Your brothers have hurt themselves by so doing. Give it up, you understand nothing about it."

But the Simpleton went on begging so long, that the father said at last,

"Well, be off with you. You will only learn by experience."

The mother gave him a cake made only with water and baked in the ashes, and with it a flask of sour beer. When he came into the forest the little old gray man met him, and greeted him, saying,

"Give me a bit of your cake, and a drink from your flask. I am so hungry and thirsty."

And the Simpleton answered, "I have only a flour and water cake and sour beer. But if that is good enough for you, let us sit down together and eat." Then they sat down, and as the

Simpleton took out his flour and water cake it became a rich pancake, and his sour beer became good wine. Then they ate and drank, and afterwards the little man said,

"As you have such a kind heart, and share what you have so willingly, I will bestow good luck upon you. Yonder stands an old tree. Cut it down, and at its roots you will find something," and thereupon the little man took his departure.

The Simpleton went there, and hewed away at the tree, and when it fell he saw, sitting among the roots, a goose with feathers of pure gold. He lifted it out and took it with him to an inn where he intended to stay the night. The landlord had three daughters who, when they saw the goose, were curious to know what wonderful kind of bird it was, and ended by longing for one of its golden feathers. The eldest thought, "I will wait for a good opportunity, and then I will pull out one of its feathers for myself." And so, when the Simpleton had gone out, she seized the goose by its wing—but there her finger and hand remained, held fast. Soon after came the second sister with the same idea of plucking out one of the golden feathers for herself. But scarcely had she touched her sister, than she also was obliged to stay, held fast. Lastly came the third with the same intentions. But the others screamed out,

"Stay away! For heaven's sake stay away!"

But she did not see why she should stay away, and thought, "If they do so, why should not I?" and went towards them. But when she reached her sisters there she stopped, hanging on with them. And so they had to stay, all night. The next morning the Simpleton took the goose under his arm and went away, unmindful of the three girls that hung on to it. The three had always to run after him, left and right, wherever his legs carried him. In the midst of the fields they met the parson, who, when he saw the procession, said,

"Shame on you, girls, running after a young fellow through the fields like this," and forthwith he seized hold of the youngest by the hand to drag her away, but hardly had he touched her when he too was obliged to run after them himself, for he was stuck to the girl. Not long after the sexton came that way, and seeing the respected parson following at the heels of the three girls, he called out,

"Ho, your reverence, whither away so quickly? You forget that we have another christening today." And he seized hold of him by his gown. But no sooner had he touched him than he was obliged to follow on too. As the five tramped on, one after another, two peasants with their hoes came up from the fields, and the parson cried out to them, and begged them to come and set him and the sexton free, but no sooner had they touched the sexton than they had to follow on too. And now there were seven following the Simpleton and the goose.

By and by they came to a town where a King reigned, who had an only daughter who was so serious that no one could make her laugh. Therefore the King had given out that whoever should make her laugh should have her in marriage. The

Simpleton, when he heard this, went with his goose and his hangers-on into the presence of the King's daughter, and as soon as she saw the seven people following always one after the other, she burst out laughing, and seemed as if she could never stop. And so the Simpleton earned a right to her as his bride. But the King did not like him for a son-in-law and made all kinds of objections, and said he must first bring a man who could drink up a whole cellar of wine. The Simpleton thought that the little gray man would be able to help him, and went out into the forest, and there, on the very spot where he felled the tree, he saw a man sitting with a very sad countenance. The Simpleton asked him what was the matter, and he answered,

"I have a great thirst, which I cannot quench for cold water does not agree with me. I have indeed drunk up a whole cask of wine, but what good is a drop like that?"

Then said the Simpleton,

"I can help you. Only come with me, and you shall have enough."

He took him straight to the King's cellar, and the man sat himself down before the big vats, and drank, and drank, and before a day was over he had drunk up the whole cellar. The Simpleton again asked for his bride, but the King was annoyed that a wretched fellow called the Simpleton should carry off his daughter, and so he made new conditions. He was to produce a man who could eat up a mountain of bread. The Simpleton did not hesitate long, but ran quickly off to the forest, and there in the same place sat a man who had fastened a strap round his body, making a very piteous face, and saying,

"I have eaten a whole bakery full of rolls, but what is the use of that when one is so hungry as I am? My stomach feels quite empty, and I am obliged to strap myself together, that I may not die of hunger."

The Simpleton was quite glad of this, and said,

"Get up quickly, and come along with me, and you shall have enough to eat."

He led him straight to the King's courtyard, where all the meal in the kingdom had been collected and baked into a mountain of bread. The man out of the forest settled himself down before it and hastened to eat, and in one day the whole mountain had disappeared.

Then the Simpleton asked for his bride the third time. The King, however, found one more excuse, and said he must have a ship that should be able to sail on land or on water.

"So soon," said he, "as you come sailing along with it, you shall have my daughter for your wife."

The Simpleton went straight to the forest, and there sat the little old gray man with whom he had shared his cake, and he said,

"I have eaten for you, and I have drunk for you, I will also give you the ship. And all because you were kind to me at the first."

Then he gave him the ship that could sail on land and on water, and when the King saw it he knew he could no longer withhold his daughter. The marriage took place immediately, and at the death of the King the Simpleton possessed the kingdom, and lived long and happily with his wife.

FAITHFUL JOHN

There was once an old King, who, having fallen sick, thought to himself, "This is very likely my deathbed on which I am lying."

Then he said, "Let Faithful John be sent for."

Faithful John was his most beloved servant, and was so called because he had served the King faithfully all his life long. When he came near the bed, the King said to him,

"Faithful John, I feel my end drawing near, and my only care is for my son. He is yet of tender years, and does not always know how to shape his conduct. Unless you promise me to instruct him in all his actions and be a true foster father to him, I shall not be able to close my eyes in peace."

Then answered Faithful John, "I will never forsake him, and will serve him faithfully, even though it should cost me my life."

And the old King said, "Then I die, being of good cheer and at peace." And he went on to say,

"After my death, you must lead him through the whole

castle, into all the chambers, halls, and vaults, and show him the treasures that in them lie. But the last chamber in the long gallery, in which lies hidden the picture of the Princess of the Golden Palace, you must not show him. If he were to see that picture, he would directly fall into so great a love for her that he would faint with the strength of it, and afterwards for her sake run into great dangers. So you must guard him well."

And as Faithful John gave him his hand upon it, the old King became still and silent, laid his head upon the pillow, and died.

When the old King was laid in the grave, Faithful John told the young prince, now the new King, what he had promised to his father on his deathbed, and said,

"And I will certainly hold to my promise and be faithful to you, as I was faithful to him, even though it should cost me my life."

When the days of mourning were at an end, Faithful John said to the young King,

"It is now time that you should see your inheritance. I will show you all the paternal castle."

Then he led him over all the place, upstairs and downstairs, and showed him all the treasures and the splendid chambers. One chamber only he did not open, that in which the perilous picture hung. Now the picture was so placed that when the door opened it was the first thing to be seen, and was so wonderfully painted that it seemed to breathe and move, and in the whole world was there nothing more lovely or more beautiful. The young King noticed how Faithful John always passed by this one door, and asked,

"Why do you not undo this door?"

"There is something inside that would terrify you," answered he. But the King answered,

"I have seen the whole castle, and I will know what is in here also." And he went forward and tried to open the door by force.

Then Faithful John called him back, and said, "I promised your father on his deathbed that you should not see what is in that room. It might bring great misfortune to you and me were I to break my promise."

But the young King answered, "I shall be undone if I do not go inside that room. I shall have no peace day or night until I have seen it with these eyes and I will not move from this place until you have unlocked it."

Then Faithful John saw there was no help for it, and he chose out the key from the big bunch with a heavy heart and many sighs. When the door was opened he walked in first, and thought that by standing in front of the King he might hide the picture from him, but that was no good, for the King stood on tiptoe and looked over his shoulder. And when he saw the image of the lady that was so wonderfully beautiful, and so glittering with gold and jewels, he fell on the ground powerless. Faithful John helped him up, took him to his bed, and thought with sorrow, "Ah me! The evil has come to pass. What will become of us?"

Then he strengthened the King with wine until he came to himself. The first words that he said were,

"Oh, the beautiful picture! Whose portrait is it?"

"It is the portrait of the Princess of the Golden Palace," answered Faithful John. Then the King said,

"My love for her is so great that if all the leaves of the forest were tongues they could not utter it! I stake my life on the chance of obtaining her, and you, my Faithful John, must stand by me."

The faithful servant considered for a long time how the business should be begun. It seemed to him that it would be a difficult matter to come only at a sight of the Princess. At last he thought out a way, and said to the King,

"All that she has about her is of gold—tables, chairs, dishes, drinking cups, bowls, and all the household furniture. In your treasury are five tons of gold. Let the goldsmiths of your kingdom work it up into all kinds of vessels and implements, into all kinds of birds, and wild creatures, and wonderful beasts, such as may please her. Then we will carry them off with us, and go and seek our fortune."

The King had all the goldsmiths fetched, and they worked day and night, until at last some splendid things were got ready. When a ship had been loaded with them, Faithful John put on the garb of a merchant, and so did the King, so as the more completely to disguise themselves. Then they journeyed over the sea, and went so far that at last they came to the city where the Princess of the Golden Palace dwelt.

Faithful John told the King to stay in the ship, and to wait for him.

"Perhaps," said he, "I shall bring the Princess back with me, so take care that everything is in order. Let the golden vessels be placed about, and the whole ship be adorned."

Then he gathered together in his apron some of the gold things, one of each kind, landed, and went up to the royal castle. And when he reached the courtyard of the castle there stood by the well a pretty maiden, who had two golden pails in her hand, and she was drawing water with them. As she turned round to carry them away she saw the strange man, and asked him who he was. He answered,

"I am a merchant," and opened his apron, and let her look within it.

"Ah, what beautiful things!" cried she, and setting down her pails, she turned the golden toys over, and looked at them one after another. Then she said,

"The Princess must see these. She takes so much pleasure in gold things that she will buy them all from you."

Then she took him by the hand and led him in, for she was the chambermaid.

When the Princess saw the golden wares she was very pleased, and said,

"All these are so finely worked that I should like to buy them of you."

But Faithful John said,

"I am only the servant of a rich merchant, and what I have here is nothing to what my master has in the ship—the cunningest and costliest things that ever were made of gold."

The Princess then wanted it all to be brought to her. But he said,

"That would take up many days. So great is the number of them, and so much space would they occupy that there would not be enough room for them in your house."

But the Princess's curiosity and fancy grew so much that at last she said,

"Lead me to the ship. I will myself go and see your master's treasures."

Then Faithful John led her to the ship joyfully, and the King, when he saw that her beauty was even greater than the picture had set forth, felt his heart leap at the sight. Then she climbed up into the ship, and the King received her. Faithful John stayed by the steersman, and gave orders for the ship to push off, saying, "Spread all sail, that she may fly like a bird in the air."

So the King showed her all the golden things, each separately—the dishes, the bowls, the birds, the wild creatures, and the wonderful beasts. Many hours were passed in looking at them all, and in her pleasure the Princess never noticed that the ship was moving onwards. When she had examined the last, she thanked the merchant, and prepared to return home. But when she came to the ship's side, she saw that they were on the high seas, far from land, and speeding on under full sail.

"Ah!" cried she, full of terror, "I am betrayed and carried off by this merchant. Oh that I had died rather than have fallen into his power!"

But the King took hold of her hand, and said,

"No merchant am I, but a King, and no baser of birth than thyself. It is because of my overpowering love for thee that I have carried thee off by cunning. The first time I saw thy picture I fell fainting to the earth."

When the Princess of the Golden Palace heard this she became more trustful, and her heart inclined favorably towards him, so that she willingly consented to become his wife.

It happened, however, as they were still journeying on the open sea, that Faithful John, as he sat in the forepart of the ship and made music, caught sight of three ravens in the air flying overhead. Then he stopped playing and listened to what they said one to another, for he understood them quite well. The first one cried,

"Ay, there goes the Princess of the Golden Palace."

"Yes," answered the second. "But he has not got her safe yet." And the third said,

"He has her, though. She sits beside him in the ship."

Then the first one spoke again,

"What does that avail him? When they come on land a red horse will spring towards them. Then will the King try to mount him. And if he does, the horse will rise with him into the air, so that he will never see his bride again." The second raven asked,

"Is there no remedy?"

"Oh yes. If another man mounts quickly, and takes the pistol out of the holster and shoots the horse dead with it, he will save the young King. But who knows that? And he that knows it and does it will become stone from toe to knee." Then said the second,

"I know further, that if the horse should be killed, the young King will not even then be sure of his bride. When they arrive at the castle there will lie a wrought shirt in a dish, and it will seem all woven of gold and silver, but it is really of sulfur and pitch, and if he puts it on it will burn him to the marrow of his bones." The third raven said,

"Is there no remedy?"

"Oh yes," answered the second. "If another man with gloves on picks up the shirt, and throws it into the fire so that it is consumed, then is the young King delivered. But what avails that? He who knows it and does it will be turned into stone from his heart to his knee." Then spoke the third,

"I know yet more, that even when the shirt is burnt up the King is not sure of his bride. When at the wedding the dance begins, and the young Queen dances, she will suddenly grow pale and fall to the earth as if she were dead, and unless someone lifts her up and takes three drops of blood from her right breast, she will die. But he that knows this and does this will become stone from the crown of his head to the sole of his foot."

When the ravens had spoken thus among themselves they flew away. Faithful John had understood it all, and from that time he remained quiet and sad, for he thought to himself that were he to conceal what he had heard from his master, misfortune would befall. And were he to discover it his own life would be sacrificed. At last, however, he said within himself,

"I will save my master, though I myself should perish!"

So when they came on land, it happened just as the ravens had foretold, there sprang forward a splendid red horse.

"Come on!" said the King. "He shall carry me to the castle." And as he was going to mount the horse, Faithful John passed before him and mounted quickly. He drew his pistol out of the holster and shot the horse dead. Then the other servants of the King cried out (for they did not wish well to Faithful John),

"How shameful to kill that beautiful animal that was to have carried the King to his castle." But the King said,

"Hold your tongues, and let him be. He is my Faithful John. He knows what is the good of it."

Then they went up to the castle, and there stood in the hall a dish, and the wrought shirt that lay on it seemed as if of gold and silver. The young King went up to it and was going to put it on, but Faithful John pushed him away, picked it up with his gloved hands, threw it quickly on the fire, and there let it burn. The other servants began grumbling again, and said,

"Look, he is even burning up the King's shirt!" But the young King said,

"Who knows but that there may be a good reason for it? Let him be, he is my Faithful John."

Then the wedding feast was held. And the bride led the dance. Faithful John watched her carefully, and all at once she grew pale and fell down as if she were dead. Then he went quickly to her, and carried her into a chamber nearby, laid her down, and kneeling, took three drops of blood from her right breast. Immediately she drew breath again and raised herself up, but the young King witnessing all, and not knowing why Faithful John had done this, grew very angry, and cried out,

"Throw him into prison!"

The next morning Faithful John was condemned to death and led to the gallows, and as he stood there ready to suffer, he said,

"He who is about to die is permitted to speak once before his end. May I claim that right?"

"Yes," answered the King, "it is granted to you." Then said Faithful John,

"I have been condemned unjustly, for I have always been faithful," and he related how he had heard on the sea voyage the talk of the ravens, and how he had done everything in order to save his master. Then cried the King,

"O my Faithful John, pardon! Pardon! Lead him down!" But Faithful John, as he spoke the last words, fell lifeless, and became stone.

The King and Queen had great grief because of this, and the King said,

"Ah, how could I have evil-rewarded such faithfulness!" And he caused the stone image to be lifted up and put to stand in his bedroom by the side of his bed. And as often as he saw it he wept and said,

"Would that I could bring thee back to life, my Faithful John!"

After some time the Queen bore twins—two little sons— who grew and thrived, and were the joy of their parents. One day, when the Queen was in church, the two children were sitting and playing with their father, and he gazed at the stone image full of sadness, sighed, and cried,

"Oh that I could bring thee back to life, my Faithful John!" Then the stone began to speak, and said,

"Yes, thou canst bring me back to life again, if thou wilt bestow therefore thy best beloved." Then cried the King,

"All that I have in the world will I give up for thee!" The stone went on to say,

"If thou wilt cut off the heads of thy two children with thy own hand, and besmear me with their blood, I shall receive life again."

The King was horror-struck at the thought that he must put his beloved children to death, but he remembered all John's faithfulness, and how he had died for him, and he drew his sword and cut off his children's heads with his own hand. And when he had besmeared the stone with their blood, life returned to it and Faithful John stood alive and well before him. And he said to the King,

"Thy faithfulness shall not be unrewarded." And, taking up the heads of the children, he set them on again, and besmeared the wound with their blood, upon which in a moment they were whole again, and jumped about, and went on playing as if nothing had happened to them.

Now was the King full of joy. And when he saw the Queen coming he put Faithful John and the two children in a great chest. When she came in he said to her,

"Hast thou prayed in church?"

"Yes," answered she, "but I was thinking all the while of Faithful John, and how he came to such great misfortune through us."

"Then," said he, "dear wife, we can give him life again, but it will cost us both our little sons, whom we must sacrifice."

The Queen grew pale and sick at heart, but said,

"We owe it him, because of his great faithfulness."

Then the King rejoiced because she thought as he did, and he went and unlocked the chest and took out the children and Faithful John, and said,

"God be praised, he is delivered, and our little sons are ours again." And he related to her how it had come to pass.

After that they all lived together in happiness to their lives' end.

THE WHITE SNAKE

A long time ago there lived a King whose wisdom was known in all the country. Nothing remained long unknown to him, and it was as if the knowledge of hidden things was brought to him in the air. However, he had one curious custom. Every day at dinner, after the table had been cleared and everyone gone away, a trusty servant had to bring in one other dish. But it was covered up, and the servant himself did not know what was in it, and no one else knew, for the King waited until he was quite alone before he uncovered it. This had gone on a long time, but at last there came a day when the servant could restrain his curiosity no longer, and as he was carrying the dish away he took it into his own room. As soon as he had fastened the door securely, he lifted the cover, and there he saw a white snake lying on the dish. After seeing it he could not resist the desire to taste it, and so he cut off a small piece and put it in his mouth. As soon as it touched his tongue he heard outside his window a strange chorus of delicate voices. He went and listened, and found that it was the sparrows talking together, and telling each other all they had seen in the fields and woods. The virtue of the snake had given him power to understand the speech of animals.

Now it happened one day that the Queen lost her most splendid ring, and suspicion fell upon the trusty servant, who had the general superintendence, and he was accused of stealing it. The King summoned him to his presence, and after many reproaches told him that if by the next day he was not able to name the thief he should be considered guilty and punished. It was in vain that he protested his innocence. He could get no better sentence. In his uneasiness and anxiety he went out into the courtyard, and began to consider what he could do in so great a necessity. There sat the ducks by the running water and rested themselves, and plumed themselves with their flat bills, and held a comfortable chat. The servant stayed where he was and listened to them. They told how they had waddled about all yesterday morning and found good food. And then one of them said pitifully,

"Something lies very heavy in my craw. It is the ring that was lying under the Queen's window. I swallowed it down in too great a hurry."

Then the servant seized her by the neck, took her into the kitchen, and said to the cook,

"Kill this one, she is quite ready for cooking."

"Yes," said the cook, weighing it in her hand. "There will be no trouble of fattening this one. It has been ready ever so long."

She then slit up its neck, and when it was opened the Queen's ring was found in its craw. The servant could now clearly prove his innocence, and in order to make up for the injustice he had suffered the King permitted him to ask some favor for himself, and also promised him the place of greatest honor in the royal household.

But the servant refused it, and only asked for a horse and money for travelling, for he had a fancy to see the world and look about him a little. So his request was granted, and he set out on his way. And one day he came to a pool of water, by which he saw three fishes who had got entangled in the rushes and were panting for water. Although fishes are usually considered dumb creatures, he understood very well their lament that they were to perish so miserably. And as he had a compassionate heart he dismounted from his horse and put the three fishes back again into the water. They quivered all over with joy, stretched out their heads, and called out to him,

"We will remember and reward thee, because thou hast delivered us." He rode on, and after a while he heard a small voice come up from the sand underneath his horse's feet. He listened, and understood how an ant king was complaining,

"If only these men would keep off, with their great awkward beasts! Here comes this stupid horse treading down my people with his hard hoofs!"

The man then turned his horse onto the side path, and the ant king called out to him,

"We will remember and reward thee!"

The path led him through a wood, and there he saw a father raven and mother raven standing by their nest and throwing their young ones out.

"Off with you, young gallows birds!" cried they. "We cannot stuff you anymore. You are big enough to fend for yourselves!" The poor young ravens lay on the ground, fluttering, and beating the air with their wings, and crying,

"We are poor helpless things, we cannot fend for ourselves, we cannot even fly! We can only die of hunger!"

Then the kind young man dismounted, killed his horse with his dagger, and left it to the young ravens for food. They came hopping up, feasted away at it, and cried,

"We will remember and reward thee!"

So now he had to use his own legs, and when he had gone a long way he came to a great town. There was much noise and thronging in the streets, and there came a man on a horse, who proclaimed,

"The King's daughter seeks a husband, but he who wishes to marry her must perform a difficult task, and if he cannot carry it through successfully, he must lose his life."

Many had already tried, but had lost their lives. The

young man, when he saw the King's daughter, was so dazzled by her great beauty that he forgot all danger, went to the King, and offered himself as a wooer.

Then he was led to the seaside, and a gold ring was thrown into the water before his eyes. Then the King told him that he must fetch the ring up again from the bottom of the sea, saying,

"If you come back without it, you shall be put under the waves again and again until you are drowned."

Everyone pitied the handsome young man, but they went, and left him alone by the sea. As he was standing on the shore and thinking of what he should do, there came three fishes swimming by, none other than those he had set free. The middle one had a mussel in his mouth, and he laid it on the sand at the young man's feet. And when he took it up and opened it there was the gold ring inside! Full of joy he carried it to the King, and expected the promised reward. But the King's daughter, proud of her high birth, despised him, and set him another task to perform. She went out into the garden, and strewed about over the grass ten sacks full of millet seed.

"By the time the sun rises in the morning you must have picked up all these," she said. "And not a grain must be wanting."

The young man sat down in the garden and considered how it was possible to do this task, but he could contrive nothing, and stayed there, feeling very sorrowful, and expecting to be led to death at break of day. But when the first beams of the sun fell on the garden he saw that the ten sacks were all filled, standing one by the other, and not even a grain was missing. The ant king had arrived in the night with his thousands of ants, and the grateful creatures had picked up all the millet seed and filled the sacks with great industry. The King's daughter came herself into the garden and saw with astonishment that the young man had performed all that had been given him to do. But she could not let her proud heart melt, but said,

"Although he has completed the two tasks, he shall not be my groom unless he brings me an apple from the tree of life."

The young man did not know where the tree of life was to be found, but he set out and went on and on, as long as his legs could carry him, but he had no hope of finding it. When he had gone through three kingdoms he came one evening to a wood, and seated himself under a tree to go to sleep. But he heard a rustling in the boughs, and a golden apple fell into his hand. Immediately three ravens flew towards him, perched on his knee, and said,

"We are the three young ravens that you delivered from starving. When we grew big and heard that you were seeking the golden apple, we flew over the sea to the end of the earth where the tree of life stands, and we fetched the apple."

Full of joy the young man set off on his way home, and brought the golden apple to the King's beautiful daughter, who was without any further excuse.

So they divided the apple of life, and ate it together. And their hearts were filled with love, and they lived in undisturbed happiness to a great age.

THE SLEEPING BEAUTY

n times past there lived a King and Queen, who said to each other every day of their lives, "Would that we had a child!" and yet they had none. But it happened once that when the Queen was bathing, there came a frog out of the water, and he squatted on the ground, and said to her,

"Thy wish shall be fulfilled. Before a year has gone by, thou shalt bring a daughter into the world."

And as the frog foretold, so it happened. And the Queen bore a daughter so beautiful that the King could not contain himself for joy, and he ordained a great feast. Not only did he bid to it his relations, friends, and acquaintances, but also the wise women, that they might be kind and favorable to the child. There were thirteen of them in his kingdom, but as he had only provided twelve golden plates for them to eat from, one of them had to be left out. However, the feast was celebrated with splendor. And as it drew to an end, the wise women stood forward to present to the child their wonderful gifts: one bestowed virtue, one beauty, a third riches, and so on, whatever there is in the world to wish for. And when eleven of them had said their say, in came the uninvited thirteenth, burning with revenge, and without greeting or respect, she cried with a loud voice,

"In the fifteenth year of her age the princess shall prick herself with a spindle and shall fall down dead."

And without speaking one more word she turned away and left the hall. Everyone was terrified at her saying, when the twelfth came forward, for she had not yet bestowed her gift, and though she could not do away with the evil prophecy, yet she could soften it, so she said,

"The princess shall not die, but fall into a deep sleep for a hundred years."

Now the King, being desirous of saving his child even from this misfortune, gave commandment that all the spindles in his kingdom should be burnt up.

The maiden grew up, adorned with all the gifts of the wise women. And she was so lovely, modest, sweet, kind, and clever, that no one who saw her could help loving her.

It happened one day, she being already fifteen years old, that the King and Queen rode abroad, and the maiden was left behind alone in the castle. She wandered about into all the nooks and corners, and into all the chambers and parlors, as the fancy took her, until at last she came to an old tower. She climbed the narrow winding stair which led to a little door, with a rusty key sticking out of the lock. She turned the key, and the door opened, and there in the little room sat an old woman with a spindle, diligently spinning her flax.

"Good day," said the princess, "what are you doing?"

"I am spinning," answered the old woman, nodding her head.

"What thing is that that twists round so briskly?" asked the maiden, and taking the spindle into her hand she began to spin. But no sooner had she touched it than the evil prophecy was fulfilled, and she pricked her finger with it. In that very moment she fell back upon the bed that stood there, and lay in a deep sleep. And this sleep fell upon the whole castle. The King and Queen, who had returned and were in the great hall, fell fast asleep, and with them the whole court. The horses in their stalls, the dogs in the yard, the pigeons on the roof, the flies on the wall, the very fire that flickered on the hearth, became still and slept like the rest. And the meat on the spit ceased roasting, and the cook, who was going to pull the scullion's hair for some mistake he had made, let him go, and went to sleep. And the wind ceased, and not a leaf fell from the trees about the castle.

Then round about that place there grew a hedge of thorns thicker every year, until at last the whole castle was hidden from view, and nothing of it could be seen but the vane on the roof. And a rumor went abroad in all that country of the beautiful sleeping Rosamond, for so was the princess called. And from time to time many Kings' sons came and tried to force their way through the hedge. But it was impossible for them to do so, for the thorns held fast together like strong hands, and the young men were caught by them, and not being able to get free, there died a lamentable death.

Many a long year afterwards there came a King's son into

that country, and heard an old man tell how there should be a castle standing behind the hedge of thorns, and that there a beautiful enchanted princess named Rosamond had slept for a hundred years, and with her the King and Queen, and the whole court. The old man had been told by his grandfather that many King's sons had sought to pass the thorn hedge, but had been caught and pierced by the thorns, and had died a miserable death. Then said the young man, "Nevertheless, I do not fear to try. I shall win through and see the lovely Rosamond." The good old man tried to dissuade him, but he would not listen to his words.

For now the hundred years were at an end, and the day had come when Rosamond should be awakened. When the prince drew near the hedge of thorns, it was changed into a hedge of beautiful large flowers, which parted and bent aside to let him pass, and then closed behind him in a thick hedge. When he reached the castle yard, he saw the horses and brindled hunting dogs lying asleep, and on the roof the pigeons were sitting with their heads under their wings. And when he came indoors, the flies on the wall were asleep, the cook in the kitchen had his hand uplifted to strike the scullion, and the kitchen maid had the black fowl on her lap ready to pluck. Then he mounted higher, and saw in the hall the whole court lying asleep, and above them, on their thrones, slept the King and the Queen. And still he went farther, and all was so quiet that he could hear his own breathing. And at last he came to the tower, and went up the winding stair, and opened the door of the little room where Rosamond lay. And when he saw her looking so lovely in her sleep, he could not turn away his eyes. And presently he stooped and kissed her, and she awaked, and opened her eyes, and looked very kindly on him. And she rose, and they went forth together, and the King and the Queen and whole court waked up, and gazed on each other with great eyes of wonderment. And the horses in the yard got up and shook themselves, the hounds sprang up and wagged their tails, the pigeons on the roof drew their heads from under their wings, looked round, and flew into the field, the flies on the wall crept on a little farther, the kitchen fire leapt up and blazed, and cooked the meat, the joint on the spit began to roast, the cook gave the scullion such a box on the ear that he roared out, and the maid went on plucking the fowl.

Then the wedding of the Prince and Rosamond was held with all splendor, and they lived very happily together until their lives' end.

THE GALLANT TAILOR

One summer morning a little tailor was sitting on his board near the window, and working cheerfully with all his might, when an old woman came down the street crying,

"Good jelly to sell! Good jelly to sell!"

The cry sounded pleasant in the little tailor's ears, so he put his head out of the window, and called out,

"Here, my good woman. Come here if you want a customer."

So the poor woman climbed the steps with her heavy basket, and was obliged to unpack and display all her pots to the tailor. He looked at every one of them, and lifting all the lids, applied his nose to each, and said at last,

"The jelly seems pretty good. You may weigh me out four half ounces, or I don't mind having a quarter of a pound."

The woman, who had expected to find a good customer, gave him what he asked for but went off angry and grumbling.

"This jelly is the very thing for me," cried the little tailor. "It will give me strength and cunning." And he took down the bread from the cupboard, cut a whole round of the loaf, spread the jelly on it, laid it near him, and went on stitching more gallantly than ever. All the while the scent of the sweet jelly was spreading throughout the room, where there were quantities of flies, who were attracted by it and flew to partake.

"Now then, who asked you to come?" said the tailor, and drove the unbidden guests away. But the flies, not understanding his language, were not to be got rid of like that, and returned in larger numbers than before. Then the tailor, not being able to stand it any longer, took from his chimney corner a ragged cloth, and saying,

"Now, I'll let you have it!" beat it among them mercilessly. When he ceased, and counted the slain, he found seven lying dead before him.

"This is indeed something," he said, wondering at his own gallantry. "The whole town shall know this."

So he hastened to cut out a belt, and he stitched it, and put on it in large capitals, "Seven at one blow!"

"The town, did I say?" said the little tailor. "The whole world shall know it!" And his heart quivered with joy, like a lamb's tail.

The tailor fastened the belt round him, and began to think of going out into the world, for his workshop seemed too small for his worship. So he looked about in all the house for something that would be useful to take with him, but he found nothing but an old cheese, which he put in his pocket. Outside the door he noticed that a bird had got caught in the bushes, so he took that and put it in his pocket with the cheese. Then he set out gallantly on his way, and as he was light and active he felt no fatigue. The way led over a mountain, and when he reached the topmost peak he saw a terrible giant sitting there. The tailor went bravely up to him, called out to him, and said,

"Comrade, good day! There you sit looking over the wide world! I am on the way thither to seek my fortune. Have you a fancy to go with me?"

The giant looked at the tailor contemptuously, and said,

"You little rascal! You miserable fellow!"

"That may be," answered the little tailor, and undoing his coat he showed the giant his belt. "You can read there whether I am a man or not!"

The giant read: "Seven at one blow!" and thinking it meant men that the tailor had killed, felt at once more respect for the little fellow. But as he wanted to prove himself, he took up a stone and squeezed it so hard that water came out of it.

"Now you can do that," said the giant. "That is, if you have the strength for it."

"That's not much," said the little tailor. "I call that play," and he put his hand in his pocket and took out the cheese and squeezed it, so that the whey ran out of it.

"Well," said he, "what do you think of that?"

The giant did not know what to say to it, for he could not have believed it of the little man. Then the giant took up a stone and threw it so high that it was nearly out of sight.

"Now, little fellow, suppose you do that!"

"Well thrown," said the tailor. "But the stone fell back to earth again. I will throw you one that will never come back." So he felt in his pocket, took out the bird, and threw it into the air. And the bird, when it found itself at liberty, took wing, flew off, and returned no more.

"What do you think of that, comrade?" asked the tailor.

"There is no doubt that you can throw," said the giant. "But we will see if you can carry."

He led the little tailor to a mighty oak tree which had been felled, and was lying on the ground, and said,

"Now, if you are strong enough, help me to carry this tree out of the wood."

"Willingly," answered the little man. "You take the trunk on your shoulders, I will take the branches with all their foliage, that is much the most difficult."

So the giant took the trunk on his shoulders, and the tailor seated himself on a branch, and the giant, who could not see what he was doing, had the whole tree to carry, and the little man on it as well. And the little man was very cheerful and merry, and whistled the tune: "*There were three tailors riding by*," as if carrying the tree was mere child's play. The giant, when he had struggled on under his heavy load a part of the way, was tired out, and cried,

"Look here, I must let go the tree!"

The tailor jumped off quickly, and taking hold of the tree with both arms, as if he were carrying it, said to the giant,

"You see you can't carry the tree though you are such a big fellow!"

They went on together a little farther, and presently they came to a cherry tree, and the giant took hold of the topmost branches, where the ripest fruit hung, and pulling them downwards, gave them to the tailor to hold, bidding him eat. But the little tailor was much too weak to hold the tree, and as the giant let go, the tree sprang back, and the tailor was caught up into the air. And when he dropped down again without any damage, the giant said to him,

"How is this? Haven't you strength enough to hold such a weak sprig as that?"

"It is not strength that is lacking," answered the little tailor. "How should it to one who has slain seven at one blow! I just jumped over the tree because the hunters are shooting down there in the bushes. You jump it too, if you can."

The giant made the attempt, and not being able to vault the tree, he remained hanging in the branches, so that once more the little tailor got the better of him. Then said the giant,

"As you are such a gallant fellow, suppose you come with me to our den, and stay the night."

The tailor was quite willing, and he followed him. When they reached the den there sat some other giants by the fire, and each had a roasted sheep in his hand and was eating it. The little tailor looked round and thought,

"There is more elbow room here than in my workshop."

And the giant showed him a bed, and told him he had better lie down upon it and go to sleep. The bed was, however, too big for the tailor, so he did not stay in it, but crept into a corner to sleep. As soon as it was midnight the giant got up, took a great staff of iron and beat the bed through with one stroke, and supposed he had made an end of that grasshopper of a tailor. Very early in the morning the giants went into the wood and forgot all about the little tailor, and when they saw him coming after them alive and merry, they were terribly frightened, and, thinking he was going to kill them, they ran away in all haste.

So the little tailor marched on, always following his nose. And after he had gone a great way he entered the courtyard belonging to a King's palace, and there he felt so overpowered with fatigue that he lay down and fell asleep. In the meanwhile came various people, who looked at him very curiously, and read on his belt, "Seven at one blow!"

"Oh!" said they. "Why should this great lord come here in time of peace? What a mighty champion he must be."

Then they went and told the King about him, and they thought that if war should break out what a worthy and useful man he would be, and that he ought not to be allowed to depart at any price. The King then summoned his council, and sent one of his courtiers to the little tailor to beg him, so soon as he should wake up, to consent to serve in the King's army. So the messenger stood and waited at the sleeper's side until his limbs began to stretch, and his eyes to open, and then he carried his answer back. And the answer was,

"That was the reason for which I came," said the little tailor, "I am ready to enter the King's service."

So he was received into it very honorably, and they built him his own house to dwell in.

But the rest of the soldiers were very much set against the little tailor, and they wished him a thousand miles away.

"What shall be done about it?" they said among themselves. "If we pick a quarrel and fight with him then seven of us will fall at each blow. That will be of no good to us."

So they came to a resolution, and went all together to the King to ask for their discharge.

"We never intended," said they, "to serve with a man who kills seven at a blow."

The King felt sorry to lose all his faithful servants because of one man, and he wished that he had never seen him, and would willingly get rid of him if he might. But he did not dare to dismiss the little tailor for fear he should kill all the King's people, and place himself upon the throne. He thought a long while about it, and at last made up his mind what to do. He sent for the little tailor, and told him that as he was so great a warrior he had a proposal to make to him. He told him that in a wood in his dominions dwelt two giants, who did great damage by robbery, murder, and fire, and that no man durst go near them for fear of his life. But that if the tailor should overcome and slay both these giants the King would give him his only daughter in marriage, and half his kingdom as dowry, and that a hundred horsemen should go with him to give him assistance.

"That would be something for a man like me!" thought the little tailor, "a beautiful princess and half a kingdom are not to be had every day," and he said to the King,

"Oh yes, I can soon overcome the giants, and yet have no need of the hundred horsemen. He who can kill seven at one blow has no need to be afraid of two."

So the little tailor set out, and the hundred horsemen followed him. When he came to the border of the wood he said to his escort,

"Stay here while I go to attack the giants."

Then he sprang into the wood, and looked about him right and left. After a while he caught sight of the two giants. They were lying down under a tree asleep, and snoring so that all the branches shook. The little tailor, all alive, filled both his pockets with stones and climbed up into the tree, and made his way to an overhanging bough, so that he could seat himself just above the sleepers. And from there he let one stone after another fall on the chest of one of the giants. For a long time the giant was quite unaware of this, but at last he awoke and pushed his comrade, and said,

"What are you hitting me for?"

"You are dreaming," said the other. "I am not touching you." And they composed themselves again to sleep, and the tailor let fall a stone on the other giant.

"What can that be?" cried he. "What are you casting at me?"

"I am casting nothing at you," answered the first, grumbling.

They disputed about it for a while, but as they were tired, they gave it up at last, and their eyes closed once more. Then the little tailor began his game anew, picked out a heavier stone and threw it down with force upon the first giant's chest.

"This is too much!" cried he, and sprang up like a madman and struck his companion such a blow that the tree shook above them. The other paid him back with ready coin, and they fought with such fury that they tore up trees by their roots to use for weapons against each other, so that at last they both of them lay dead upon the ground. And now the little tailor got down.

"Another piece of luck!" said he. "That the tree I was sitting in did not get torn up too, or else I should have had to jump like a squirrel from one tree to another."

Then he drew his sword and gave each of the giants a few hacks in the breast, and went back to the horsemen and said,

"The deed is done, I have made an end of both of them, but it went hard with me. In the struggle they rooted up trees to defend themselves, but it was of no use. They had to deal with a man who can kill seven at one blow."

"Then are you not wounded?" asked the horsemen.

"Nothing of the sort!" answered the tailor. "I have not turned a hair."

The horsemen still would not believe it, and rode into the wood to see, and there they found the giants wallowing in their blood, and all about them lying the uprooted trees.

The little tailor then claimed the promised boon, but the King repented him of his offer, and he sought again how to rid himself of the hero.

"Before you can possess my daughter and the half of my kingdom," said he to the tailor, "you must perform another heroic act. In the wood lives a unicorn who does great damage. You must secure him."

"A unicorn does not strike more terror into me than two giants. Seven at one blow! That is my way," was the tailor's answer.

So, taking a rope and an axe with him, he went out into the wood, and told those who were ordered to attend him to wait outside. He had not far to seek, for the unicorn soon came out and sprang at him, as if he would make an end of

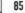

him without delay. "Softly, softly," said he. "Most haste, worst speed," and remained standing until the animal came quite near, then he slipped quietly behind a tree. The unicorn ran with all his might against the tree and stuck his horn so deep into the trunk that he could not get it out again, and so was taken.

"Now I have you," said the tailor, coming out from behind the tree, and, putting the rope round the unicorn's neck, he took the axe, set free the horn, and when all his party were assembled he led forth the animal and brought it to the King.

The King did not yet wish to give him the promised reward, and set him a third task to do. Before the wedding could take place the tailor was to secure a wild boar which had done a great deal of damage in the wood.

The huntsmen were to accompany him.

"All right," said the tailor. "This is child's play."

But he did not take the huntsmen into the wood, and they were all the better pleased, for the wild boar had many a time before received them in such a way that they had no fancy to disturb him. When the boar caught sight of the tailor he ran at him with foaming mouth and gleaming tusks to bear him to the ground, but the nimble hero rushed into a chapel which chanced to be near, and jumped quickly out of a window on the other side. The boar ran after him, and when he got inside the door shut after him, and there he was imprisoned, for the creature was too big and unwieldy to jump out of the window too. Then the little tailor called the huntsmen that they might see the prisoner with their own eyes. And then he betook himself to the King, who now, whether he liked it or not, was obliged to fulfill his promise, and give him his daughter and the half of his kingdom. But if he had known that the great warrior was only a little tailor he would have taken it still more to heart. So the wedding was celebrated with great splendor and little joy, and the tailor was made into a King.

One night the young Queen heard her husband talking in his sleep and saying,

"Now boy, make me that waistcoat and patch me those breeches, or I will lay my yard measure about your shoulders!"

And so, as she perceived of what low birth her husband was, she went to her father the next morning and told him all, and begged him to set her free from a man who was nothing better than a tailor. The King bade her be comforted, saying,

"Tonight leave your bedroom door open, my guards shall stand outside, and when he is asleep they shall come in and bind him and carry him off to a ship, and he shall be sent to the other side of the world."

So the wife felt consoled, but the King's water bearer, who had been listening all the while, went to the little tailor and disclosed to him the whole plan.

"I shall put a stop to all this," said he.

At night he lay down as usual in bed, and when his wife thought that he was asleep, she got up, opened the door and lay down again. The little tailor, who only made believe to be asleep, began to murmur plainly,

"Now, boy, make me that waistcoat and patch me those breeches, or I will lay my yard measure about your shoulders! I have slain seven at one blow, killed two giants, caught a unicorn, and taken a wild boar, and shall I be afraid of those who are standing outside my room door?"

And when they heard the tailor say this, a great fear seized the guards. They fled away as if they had been wild hares, and none of them would venture to attack him.

And so the little tailor all his lifetime remained a King.

KING THRUSHBEARD

A King had a daughter who was beautiful beyond measure, but so proud and overbearing that none of her suitors were good enough for her. She not only refused one after the other, but made a laughing-stock of them. Once the king appointed a great feast, and bade all the marriageable men to it from far and near. And they were all put in rows, according to their rank and station. First came the Kings, then the princes, the dukes, the earls, the barons, and lastly the noblemen. The princess was led in front of the rows, but she had a mocking epithet for each. One was too fat: "What a tub!" said she. Another too tall: "Long and lean is ill to be seen," said she. A third too short: "Fat and short, not fit to court," said she. A fourth was too pale: "A regular death's head." A fifth too red-faced: "A gamecock," she called him. The sixth was not well made enough: "Green wood ill dried!" cried she. So everyone had something against him, and she made especially merry over a good King who was very tall, and whose chin had grown a little peaked.

"Only look," cried she, laughing. "He has a chin like a thrush's beak."

And from that time they called him King Thrushbeard. But the old King, when he saw that his daughter mocked everyone, and scorned all the assembled suitors, swore in his anger that she should have the first beggar that came to the door for a husband.

A few days afterwards came a travelling singer, and sang under the window in hopes of a small alms. When the King heard of it, he said that he must come in. And so the singer entered in his dirty tattered garments, and sang before the King and his daughter. When he had done, he asked for a small reward. But the King said,

"Thy song has so well pleased me, that I will give thee my daughter to wed."

The princess was horrified. But the King said,

"I took an oath to give you to the first beggar that came, and so it must be done."

There was no remedy. The priest was fetched, and she had to be married to the singer out of hand. When all was done, the King said,

"Now, as you are a beggar's wife, you can stay no longer in my castle, so off with you and your husband."

The beggar led her away, and she was obliged to go forth with him on foot. On the way they came to a great wood, and she asked,

"Oh, whose is this forest, so thick and so fine?"

He answered,

"It is King Thrushbeard's, and might have been thine."

And she cried,

"Oh, I was a silly young thing, I'm afeared,
Would I had taken that good King Thrushbeard!"

Then they passed through a meadow, and she asked,

"Oh, whose is this meadow, so green and so fine?"

He answered,

"It is King Thrushbeard's, and might have been thine."

And she cried,

"I was a silly young thing, I'm afeared,
Would I had taken that good King Thrushbeard!"

Then they passed through a great town, and she asked,

"Whose is this city, so great and so fine?"

He answered,

"Oh, it is King Thrushbeard's, and might have been
    thine."

And she cried,

"I was a silly young thing, I'm afeared,
Would I had taken that good King Thrushbeard!"

Then said the beggar,
"It does not please me to hear you always wishing for an-other husband. Am I not good enough for you?"

At last they came to a very small house, and she said,

"Oh dear me! What poor little house do I see?
And whose, I would know, may the wretched hole
    be?"

The man answered,
"That is my house and thine, where we must live to-gether."

She had to stoop before she could go in at the door.

"Where are the servants?" asked the King's daughter.

"What servants?" answered the beggar. "What you want to have done you must do yourself. Make a fire quick, and put on water, and cook me some food. I am very tired."

But the King's daughter understood nothing about fire-making and cooking, and the beggar had to lend a hand himself in order to manage it at all. And when they had eaten their poor fare, they went to bed. But the man called up his wife very early in the morning, in order to clean the house. For a few days they lived in this indifferent manner, until they came to the end of their store.

"Wife," said the man, "this will not do, stopping here and earning nothing. You must make baskets."

So he went out and cut willows, and brought them home. And she began to weave them, but the hard twigs wounded her tender hands.

"I see this will not do," said the man. "You had better try spinning."

So she sat down and tried to spin, but the harsh thread cut her soft fingers, so that the blood flowed.

"Look now!" said the man. "You are no good at any sort of work. I made a bad bargain when I took you. I must see what I can do to make a trade of pots and earthen vessels. You can sit in the market and offer them for sale."

"Oh dear!" thought she. "Suppose while I am selling in

the market people belonging to my father's kingdom should see me, how they would mock at me!"

But there was no help for it. She had to submit, or else die of hunger.

The first day all went well. The people bought her wares eagerly, because she was so beautiful, and gave her whatever she asked, and some of them gave her the money and left the pots after all behind them. And they lived on these earnings as long as they lasted. And then the man bought a number of new pots. So she seated herself in a corner of the market, and stood the wares before her for sale. All at once a drunken soldier on horseback came plunging by, and rode straight into the midst of her pots, breaking them into a thousand pieces. She could do nothing for weeping.

"Oh dear, what will become of me," cried she. "What will my husband say?" and she hastened home and told him her misfortune.

"Whoever heard of such a thing as sitting in the corner of the market with earthenware pots!" said the man. "Now leave off crying. I see you are not fit for any regular work. I have been asking at your father's castle if they want a kitchen-maid, and they say they don't mind taking you. At any rate you will get your victuals free."

And the King's daughter became a kitchen-maid, to be at the cook's beck and call, and to do the hardest work. In each of her pockets she fastened a little pot, and brought home in them whatever was left, and upon that she and her husband were fed. It happened one day, when the wedding of the eldest prince was celebrated, the poor woman went upstairs, and stood by the parlor door to see what was going on. And when the place was lighted up, and the company arrived, each person handsomer than the one before, and all was brilliancy and splendor, she thought on her own fate with a sad heart, and bewailed her former pride and haughtiness which had brought her so low, and plunged her in such great poverty. And as the rich and delicate dishes smelling so good were carried to and fro every now and then, the servants would throw her a few fragments, which she put in her pockets, intending to take home. And then the prince himself passed in clothed in silk and velvet, with a gold chain round his neck. And when he saw the beautiful woman standing in the doorway, he seized her hand and urged her to dance with him, but she refused, all trembling, for she saw it was King Thrushbeard, who had come to court her, whom she had turned away with mocking. It was of no use her resisting, for he drew her into the room. And all at once the band to which her pockets were fastened broke, and the pots fell out, and the soup ran about, and the fragments were scattered all round. And when the people saw that, there was great laughter and mocking, and she felt so ashamed, that she wished herself a thousand fathoms underground. She rushed to the door to fly from the place, when a man caught her just on the steps, and when she looked at him, it was King Thrushbeard again. He said to her in a kind tone,

"Do not be afraid, I and the beggar with whom you lived in the wretched little hut are one and the same. For love of you I disguised myself, and it was I who broke your pots in the guise of a soldier. I did all that to bring down your proud heart, and to punish your haughtiness, which caused you to mock at me." Then she wept bitterly, and said,

"I have done great wrong, and am not worthy to be your wife."

But he said,

"Take courage, the evil days are gone over. Now let us keep our wedding day."

Then came the ladies-in-waiting and put on her splendid clothing. And her father came, and the whole court, and wished her joy on her marriage with King Thrushbeard. And then the merrymaking began in good earnest. I cannot help wishing that you and I could have been there too.

THE BREMEN TOWN MUSICIANS

There was once a donkey whose master had made him carry sacks to the mill for many a long year, but whose strength began at last to fail, so that each day as it came found him less capable of work. Then his master began to think of turning him out, but the donkey, guessing that something was in the wind that boded him no good, ran away, taking the road to Bremen. For there he thought he might get an engagement as town musician. When he had gone a little way he found a hound lying by the side of the road panting, as if he had run a long way.

"What are you so out of breath about?" said the donkey.

"Oh dear!" said the dog. "Now I am old, I get weaker every day, and can do no good in the hunt, so, as my master was going to have me killed, I have made my escape. But now, how am I to gain a living?"

"I will tell you what," said the donkey. "I am going to Bremen to become town musician. You may as well go with me, and take up music too. I can play the lute, and you can beat the drum."

And the dog consented, and they walked on together. It was not long before they came to a cat sitting in the road, looking as dismal as three wet days.

"Now then, what is the matter with you?" said the donkey.

"I should like to know who would be cheerful when his neck is in danger?" answered the cat. "Now that I am old my teeth are getting blunt, and I would rather sit by the oven and purr than run about after mice, and my mistress wanted to drown me. So I took myself off. But good advice is scarce, and I do not know what is to become of me."

"Go with us to Bremen," said the donkey. "Become town musician. You understand serenading."

The cat thought well of the idea, and went with them accordingly. After that the three travelers passed by a yard, and a rooster was perched on the gate crowing with all his might.

"Your cries are enough to pierce bone and marrow," said the donkey. "What is the matter?"

"I have foretold good weather for Lady day, so that all the shirts may be washed and dried. And now on Sunday morning company is coming, and the mistress has told the cook that I must be made into soup, and this evening my neck is to be wrung, so that I am crowing with all my might while I can."

"You had much better go with us, Chanticleer," said the donkey. "We are going to Bremen. At any rate that will be better than dying. You have a powerful voice, and when we are all performing together it will have a very good effect."

So the rooster consented, and they went on all four together.

But Bremen was too far off to be reached in one day, and towards evening they came to a wood, where they determined to pass the night. The donkey and the dog lay down under a large tree. The cat got up among the branches, and the rooster flew up to the top, as that was the safest place for him. Before he went to sleep he looked all round him to the four points of the compass, and perceived in the distance a little light shining, and he called out to his companions that there must be a house not far off, as he could see a light, so the donkey said,

"We had better get up and go there, for these are uncomfortable quarters." The dog began to fancy a few bones, not quite bare, would do him good. And they all set off in the direction of the light, and it grew larger and brighter, until at last it led them to a robber's house, all lit up. The donkey, being the biggest, went up to the window, and looked in.

"Well, what do you see?" asked the dog.

"What do I see?" answered the donkey. "Here is a table set out with splendid food and drink, and robbers sitting at it and making themselves very comfortable."

"That would just suit us," said the rooster.

"Yes, indeed, I wish we were there," said the donkey. Then they consulted together how it should be managed so as to get the robbers out of the house, and at last they hit on a plan. The donkey was to place his forefeet on the windowsill, the dog was to get on the donkey's back, the cat on the top of the dog, and lastly the rooster was to fly up and perch on the cat's head. When that was done, at a given signal they all began to perform their music. The donkey brayed, the dog barked, the cat mewed, and the rooster crowed. Then they burst through into the room, breaking all the panes of glass. The robbers fled at the dreadful sound. They thought it was some goblin, and fled to the wood in the utmost terror. Then the four companions sat down to table, made free with the remains of the meal, and feasted as if they had been hungry for a month. And when they had finished they put out the lights, and each sought out a sleeping place to suit his nature and habits. The donkey laid himself down outside on the dunghill, the dog behind the door, the cat on the hearth by the warm ashes, and the rooster settled himself in the loft, and as they were all tired with their long journey they soon fell fast asleep.

When midnight drew near, and the robbers from afar saw that no light was burning, and that everything appeared quiet, their captain said to them that he thought that they had run away without reason, telling one of them to go and reconnoiter. So one of them went, and found everything quite quiet. He went into the kitchen to strike a light, and taking the glowing fiery eyes of the cat for burning coals, he held a match to them in order to kindle it. But the cat, not seeing the joke, flew into his face, spitting and scratching. Then the robber cried out in terror, and ran to get out at the back door, but the dog, who was lying there, ran at him and bit his leg. And as he was rushing through the yard by the dunghill the donkey struck out and gave him a great kick with his hind foot. And the rooster, who had been wakened with the noise, and felt quite brisk, cried out, "Cock-a-doodle-doo!"

Then the robber got back as well as he could to his captain, and said, "Oh dear! In that house there is a gruesome witch, and I felt her breath and her long nails in my face. And by the door there stands a man who stabbed me in the leg with a knife. And in the yard there lies a black specter, who beat me with his wooden club. And above, upon the roof, there sits the justice, who cried, 'Bring that rogue here!' And so I ran away from the place as fast as I could."

From that time forward the robbers never ventured to that house, and the four Bremen town musicians found themselves so well off where they were, that there they stayed. And the person who last related this tale is still living, as you see.

HANS IN LUCK

Hans had served his master seven years, and at the end of the seventh year he said,

"Master, my time is up. I want to go home and see my mother, so give me my wages."

"You have served me truly and faithfully," said the master. "As the service is, so must the wages be," and he gave him a lump of gold as big as his head. Hans pulled his handkerchief out of his pocket and tied up the lump of gold in it, hoisted it on his shoulder, and set off on his way home. And as he was trudging along, there came in sight a man riding on a spirited horse, and looking very gay and lively. "Oh!" cried Hans aloud. "How splendid riding must be! Sitting as much at one's ease as in an armchair, stumbling over no stones, saving one's shoes, and getting on one hardly knows how!"

The horseman heard Hans say this, and called out to him, "Well Hans, what are you doing on foot?"

"I can't help myself," said Hans. "I have this great lump

to carry. To be sure, it is gold, but then I can't hold my head straight for it, and it hurts my shoulder."

"I'll tell you what," said the horseman. "We will change. I will give you my horse, and you shall give me your lump of gold."

"With all my heart," said Hans. "But I warn you, you will find it heavy." And the horseman got down, took the gold, and, helping Hans up, he gave the reins into his hand.

"When you want to go fast," said he, "you must click your tongue and cry 'Gee-up!'"

And Hans, as he sat upon his horse, was glad at heart, and rode off with merry cheer. After a while he thought he should like to go quicker, so he began to click with his tongue and to cry "Gee-up!" And the horse began to trot, and Hans was thrown before he knew what was going to happen, and there he lay in the ditch by the side of the road. The horse would have got away but that he was caught by a peasant who was passing that way and driving a cow before him. And Hans pulled himself together and got upon his feet, feeling very vexed. "Poor work, riding," said he. "Especially on a jade like this, who starts off and throws you before you know where you are, going near to break your neck. Never shall I try that game again. Now, your cow is something worth having, one can jog on comfortably after her and have her milk, butter, and cheese every day, into the bargain. What would I not give to have such a cow!"

"Well now," said the peasant. "Since it will be doing you such a favor, I don't mind exchanging my cow for your horse."

Hans agreed most joyfully, and the peasant, swinging himself into the saddle, was soon out of sight.

And Hans went along driving his cow quietly before him, and thinking all the while of the fine bargain he had made.

"With only a piece of bread I shall have everything I can possibly want, for I shall always be able to have butter and cheese to it, and if I am thirsty I have nothing to do but to milk my cow. And what more is there for heart to wish!"

And when he came to an inn he made a halt, and in the joy of his heart ate up all the food he had brought with him, dinner and supper and all, and bought half a glass of beer with his last two farthings. Then on he went again driving his cow, until he should come to the village where his mother lived. It was now near the middle of the day, and the sun grew hotter and hotter, and Hans found himself on a heath which it would be an hour's journey to cross. And he began to feel very hot, and so thirsty that his tongue clove to the roof of his mouth.

"Never mind," said Hans. "I can find a remedy. I will milk my cow at once." And tying her to a dry tree, and taking off his leather cap to serve for a pail, he began to milk, but not a drop came. And as he set to work rather awkwardly, the impatient beast gave him such a kick on the head with his hind foot that he fell to the ground, and for some time could not think where he was. Then luckily there came by a butcher who was wheeling along a young pig in a wheelbarrow.

"Here's a fine piece of work!" cried he, helping poor Hans on his legs again. Then Hans related to him all that had happened. And the butcher handed him his flask, saying,

"Here, take a drink, and be a man again. Of course the cow would give no milk. She is old and only fit to draw burdens, or to be slaughtered."

"Well, to be sure," said Hans, scratching his head. "Who would have thought it? Of course it is a very handy way of getting meat when a man has a beast of his own to kill. But for my part I do not care much about cow beef, it is rather tasteless. Now, if I had but a young pig, that is much better meat, and then the sausages!"

"Look here, Hans," said the butcher. "Just for love of you I will exchange, and will give you my pig instead of your cow."

"Heaven reward such kindness!" cried Hans, and handing over the cow, received in exchange the pig, who was turned out of his wheelbarrow and was to be led by a string.

So on went Hans, thinking how everything turned out according to his wishes, and how, if trouble overtook him, all was sure to be set right directly. After a while he fell in with a peasant, who was carrying a fine white goose under his arm. They bid each other good day, and Hans began to tell about his luck, and how he had made so many good exchanges. And the peasant told how he was taking the goose to a christening feast.

"Just feel how heavy it is," said he, taking it up by the wings. "It has been fattening for the last eight weeks. And when it is roasted, won't the fat run down!"

"Yes, indeed," said Hans, weighing it in his hand. "Very fine to be sure. But my pig is not to be despised."

Upon which the peasant glanced cautiously on all sides, and shook his head.

"I am afraid," said he, "that there is something not quite right about your pig. In the village I have just left one had actually been stolen from the bailiff's yard. I fear, I fear you have it in your hand. They have sent after the thief, and it would be bad for you if it was found upon you. The least that could happen would be to be thrown into a dark hole."

Poor Hans grew pale with fright. "For heaven's sake," said he. "Help me out of this scrape, I am a stranger in these parts. Take my pig and give me your goose."

"It will be running some risk," answered the man. "But I will do it sooner than that you should come to grief." And so, taking the cord in his hand, he drove the pig quickly along a path, and lucky Hans went on his way home with the goose under his arm. "The more I think of it," said he to himself, "the better the bargain seems. First I get the roast goose. Then the fat. That will last a whole year for bread and dripping. And lastly the beautiful white feathers which I can stuff my pillow with. How comfortably I shall sleep upon it, and how pleased my mother will be!"

And when he reached the last village, he saw a knife grinder with his barrow. And his wheel went whirring round, and he sang,

> "My scissors I grind, and my wheel I turn.
> And all good fellows my trade should learn,
> For all that I meet with just serves my turn."

And Hans stood and looked at him. And at last he spoke to him and said,

"You seem very well off, and merry with your grinding."

"Yes," answered the knife grinder. "My handiwork pays very well. I call a man a good grinder who, every time he puts his hand in his pocket finds money there. But where did you buy that fine goose?"

"I did not buy it, but I exchanged it for my pig," said Hans.

"And the pig?"

"That I exchanged for a cow."

"And the cow?"

"That I exchanged for a horse."

"And the horse?"

"I gave for the horse a lump of gold as big as my head."

"And the gold?"

"Oh, that was my wage for seven years' service."

"You seem to have fended for yourself very well," said the knife grinder. "Now, if you could but manage to have money in your pocket every time you put your hand in, your fortune is made."

"How shall I manage that?" said Hans.

"You must be a knife grinder like me," said the man. "All you want is a grindstone, the rest comes of itself: I have one here. To be sure it is a little damaged, but I don't mind letting you have it in exchange for your goose. What say you?"

"How can you ask?" answered Hans. "I shall be the luckiest fellow in the world, for if I find money whenever I put my hand in my pocket, there is nothing more left to want."

And so he handed over the goose to the peddler and received the grindstone in exchange.

"Now," said the knife grinder, taking up a heavy common stone that lay near him. "Here is another proper sort of stone that will stand a good deal of wear and that you can hammer out your old nails upon. Take it with you, and carry it carefully."

Hans lifted up the stone and carried it off with a contented mind. "I must have been born under a lucky star!" cried he, while his eyes sparkled for joy. "I have only to wish for a thing and it is mine."

After a while he began to feel rather tired, as indeed he had been on his legs since daybreak. He also began to feel rather hungry, as in the fullness of his joy at getting the cow, he had eaten up all he had. At last he could scarcely go on at all, and had to make a halt every moment, for the stones weighed him down most unmercifully, and he could not help wishing that he did not feel obliged to drag them along. And on he went at a snail's pace until he came to a well. Then he thought he would rest and take a drink of the fresh water. And he placed the stones carefully by his side at the edge of the well. Then he sat down, and as he stooped to drink, he happened to give the stones a little push, and they both fell into the water with a splash. And then Hans, having watched them disappear, jumped for joy, and thanked his stars that he had been so lucky as to get rid of the stones that had weighed upon him so long without any effort of his own.

"I really think," cried he, "I am the luckiest man under the sun." So on he went, void of care, until he reached his mother's house.

RUMPELSTILTSKIN

There was once a miller who was poor, but he had one beautiful daughter. It happened one day that he came to speak with the King, and, to give himself consequence, he told him that he had a daughter who could spin gold out of straw. The King said to the miller,

"That is an art that pleases me well. If thy daughter is as clever as you say, bring her to my castle tomorrow, that I may put her to the proof."

When the girl was brought to him, he led her into a room that was quite full of straw, and gave her a wheel and spindle, and said,

"Now set to work, and if by the early morning thou hast not spun this straw to gold thou shalt die." And he shut the door himself, and left her there alone.

And so the poor miller's daughter was left there sitting, and could not think what to do for her life. She had no notion how to set to work to spin gold from straw, and her distress grew so great that she began to weep. Then all at once the door opened, and in came a little man, who said,

"Good evening, miller's daughter. Why are you crying?"

"Oh!" answered the girl. "I have got to spin gold out of straw, and I don't understand the business."

Then the little man said,

"What will you give me if I spin it for you?"

"My necklace," said the girl.

The little man took the necklace, seated himself before the wheel, and whirr, whirr, whirr! Three times round and the bobbin was full. Then he took up another, and whirr, whirr, whirr! Three times round, and that was full. And so he went on until the morning, when all the straw had been spun, and all the bobbins were full of gold. At sunrise came the King, and when he saw the gold he was astonished and very much rejoiced, for he was very avaricious. He had the miller's daughter taken into another room filled with straw, much bigger than the last, and told her that as she valued her life she must spin it all in one night. The girl did not know what to do, so she began to cry, and then the door opened, and the little man appeared and said,

"What will you give me if I spin all this straw into gold?"

"The ring from my finger," answered the girl.

So the little man took the ring, and began again to send the wheel whirring round, and by the next morning all the straw was spun into glistening gold. The King was rejoiced beyond measure at the sight, but as he could never have enough of gold, he had the miller's daughter taken into a still larger room full of straw, and said,

"This, too, must be spun in one night, and if you accomplish it you shall be my wife." For he thought, "Although she is but a miller's daughter, I am not likely to find anyone richer in the whole world."

As soon as the girl was left alone, the little man appeared for the third time and said,

"What will you give me if I spin the straw for you this time?"

"I have nothing left to give," answered the girl.

"Then you must promise me the first child you have after you are Queen," said the little man.

"But who knows whether that will happen?" thought the girl. But as she did not know what else to do in her necessity, she promised the little man what he desired, upon which he began to spin, until all the straw was gold. And when in the morning the King came and found all done according to his wish, he caused the wedding to be held at once, and the miller's pretty daughter became Queen.

In a year's time she brought a fine child into the world, and thought no more of the little man. But one day he came suddenly into her room, and said,

"Now give me what you promised me."

The Queen was terrified greatly, and offered the little man all the riches of the kingdom if he would only leave the child. But the little man said,

"No, I would rather have something living than all the treasures of the world."

Then the Queen began to lament and to weep, so that the little man had pity upon her.

"I will give you three days," said he. "And if at the end of that time you cannot tell my name, you must give up the child to me."

Then the Queen spent the whole night in thinking over all the names that she had ever heard, and sent a messenger through the land to ask far and wide for all the names that could be found. And when the little man came next day, (beginning with Caspar, Melchior, Balthazar) she repeated all she knew, and went through the whole list, but after each the little man said,

"That is not my name."

The second day the Queen sent to inquire of all the neighbors what the servants were called, and told the little man all the most unusual and singular names, saying,

"Perhaps you are called Roast-ribs, or Sheepshanks, or Spindleshanks?" But he answered nothing but

"That is not my name."

The third day the messenger came back again, and said,

"I have not been able to find one single new name. But as I passed through the woods I came to a high hill, and near it was a little house, and before the house burned a fire, and round the fire danced a comical little man, and he hopped on one leg and cried,

"Today do I bake, tomorrow I brew,
The day after that the Queen's child comes in.
And oh! I am glad that nobody knew
That the name I am called is Rumpelstiltskin!"

You cannot think how pleased the Queen was to hear that name, and soon afterwards, when the little man walked in and said, "Now, Mrs. Queen, what is my name?" she said at first,

"Are you called Jack?"

"No," answered he.

"Are you called Harry?" she asked again.

"No," answered he. And then she said,

"Then perhaps your name is Rumpelstiltskin!"

"The devil told you that! The devil told you that!" cried the little man, and in his anger he stamped with his right foot so hard that it went into the ground above his knee. Then he seized his left foot with both his hands in such a fury that he split in two, and there was an end of him.

OLD SULTAN

There was once a peasant who owned a faithful dog called Sultan, now grown so old that he had lost all his teeth, and could lay hold of nothing. One day the man was standing at the door of his house with his wife, and he said,

"I shall kill old Sultan tomorrow. He is of no good any longer."

His wife felt sorry for the poor dog, and answered, "He has served us for so many years, and has kept with us so faithfully, he deserves food and shelter in his old age."

"Dear me, you do not seem to understand the matter," said the husband. "He has never a tooth, and no thief would mind him in the least, so I do not see why he should not be made away with. If he has served us well, we have given him plenty of good food."

The poor dog, who was lying stretched out in the sun not far off, heard all they said, and was very sad to think that the next day would be his last. He bethought him of his great friend the wolf, and slipped out in the evening to the wood to see him, and related to him the fate that was awaiting him.

"Listen to me, old fellow," said the wolf. "Be of good courage, I will help you in your need. I have thought of a way. Early tomorrow morning your master is going to harvest the hay with his wife, and they will take their child with them, so that no one will be left at home. They will be sure to lay the child in the shade behind the hedge while they are at work. You must lie by its side, just as if you were watching it. Then I will come out of the wood and steal away the child. You must rush after me, as if to save it from me. Then I must let it fall, and you must bring it back again to its parents, who will think that you have saved it, and will be much too grateful to do you any harm. On the contrary, you will be received into full favor, and they will never let you want for anything again."

The dog was pleased with the plan, which was carried out accordingly. When the father saw the wolf running away with his child he cried out, and when old Sultan brought it back again, he was much pleased with him, and patted him, saying,

"Not a hair of him shall be touched. He shall have food and shelter as long as he lives." And he said to his wife,

"Go home directly and make some good stew for old Sultan, something that does not need biting. And get the pillow from my bed for him to lie on."

From that time old Sultan was made so comfortable that

he had nothing left to wish for. Before long the wolf paid him a visit, to congratulate him that all had gone so well.

"But, old fellow," said he, "you must wink at my making off by chance with a fat sheep of your master's. Perhaps one will escape some fine day."

"Don't reckon on that," answered the dog. "I cannot consent to it. I must remain true to my master."

But the wolf, not supposing it was said in earnest, came sneaking in the night to carry off the sheep. But the master, who had been warned by the faithful Sultan of the wolf's intention, was waiting for him, and gave him a fine hiding with the threshing flail. So the wolf had to make his escape, calling out to the dog,

"You shall pay for this, you traitor!"

The next morning the wolf sent the wild boar to call out the dog and to appoint a meeting in the wood to receive satisfaction from him. Old Sultan could find no second but a cat with three legs. And as they set off together, the poor thing went limping along, holding her tail up in the air. The wolf and his second were already on the spot. When they saw their antagonists coming, and caught sight of the elevated tail of the cat, they thought it was a saber they were bringing with them. And as the poor thing came limping on three legs, they supposed it was lifting a big stone to throw at them. This frightened them very much. The wild boar crept among the leaves, and the wolf clambered up into a tree. And when the dog and cat came up, they were surprised not to see anyone there. However, the wild boar was not perfectly hidden in the leaves, and the tips of his ears peeped out. And when the cat caught sight of one, she thought it was a mouse, and sprang upon it, seizing it with her teeth. Out leaped the wild boar with a dreadful cry, and ran away shouting,

"There is the culprit in the tree!"

And the dog and the cat looking up caught sight of the wolf, who came down, quite ashamed of his timidity, and made peace with the dog once more.

THE WOLF AND THE
SEVEN LITTLE GOATS

There was once an old goat who had seven little ones, and was as fond of them as ever mother was of her children. One day she had to go into the wood to fetch food for them, so she called them all round her.

"Dear children," said she, "I am going out into the wood. And while I am gone, be on your guard against the wolf, for if he were once to get inside he would eat you up, skin, bones, and all. The wretch often disguises himself, but he may always be known by his hoarse voice and black paws."

"Dear mother," answered the kids, "you need not be afraid, we will take good care of ourselves." And the mother bleated good-bye, and went on her way with an easy mind.

It was not long before someone came knocking at the house door, and crying out,

"Open the door, my dear children, your mother is come back, and has brought each of you something."

But the little kids knew it was the wolf by the hoarse voice.

"We will not open the door," cried they. "You are not our mother, she has a delicate and sweet voice, and your voice is hoarse. You must be the wolf."

Then off went the wolf to a shop and bought a big lump of chalk, and ate it up to make his voice soft. And then he came back, knocked at the house door, and cried,

"Open the door, my dear children, your mother is here, and has brought each of you something."

But the wolf had put up his black paws against the window, and the kids, seeing this, cried out,

"We will not open the door. Our mother has no black paws like you. You must be the wolf."

The wolf then ran to a baker.

"Baker," said he, "I am hurt in the foot. Pray spread some dough over the place."

And when the baker had plastered his feet, he ran to the miller.

"Miller," said he, "strew me some white meal over my paws." But the miller refused, thinking the wolf must be meaning harm to someone.

"If you don't do it," cried the wolf, "I'll eat you up!"

And the miller was afraid and did as he was told. And that just shows what men are.

And now came the rogue the third time to the door and knocked. "Open, children!" cried he. "Your dear mother has come home, and brought you each something from the wood."

"First show us your paws," said the kids, "so that we may know if you are really our mother or not."

And he put up his paws against the window, and when they saw that they were white, all seemed right, and they opened the door. And when he was inside they saw it was the wolf, and they were terrified and tried to hide themselves. One ran under the table, the second got into the bed, the third into the oven, the fourth in the kitchen, the fifth in the cupboard, the sixth under the sink, the seventh in the clock case. But the wolf found them all, and gave them short shrift. One after the other he swallowed down, all but the youngest, who was hid in the clock case. And so the wolf, having got what he wanted, strolled forth into the green meadows, and laying himself down under a tree, he fell asleep.

Not long after, the mother goat came back from the wood. And, oh! What a sight met her eyes! The door was standing wide open, table, chairs, and stools, all thrown about, dishes broken, quilt and pillows torn off the bed. She sought her children, but they were nowhere to be found. She called to each of them by name, but nobody answered, until she came to the name of the youngest.

"Here I am, mother," a little voice cried. "Here, in the clock case."

And so she helped him out, and heard how the wolf had come, and eaten all the rest. And you may think how she cried for the loss of her dear children. At last in her grief she wandered out of doors, and the youngest kid with her. And when they came into the meadow, there they saw the wolf lying under a tree, and snoring so that the branches shook. The mother goat looked at him carefully on all sides and she noticed how something inside his body was moving and struggling.

"Dear me!" thought she. "Can it be that my poor children that he devoured for his evening meal are still alive?" And she sent the little kid back to the house for a pair of shears, and needle, and thread. Then she cut the wolf's body open, and no sooner had she made one snip than out came the head of one of the kids, and then another snip, and then one after the other the six little kids all jumped out alive and well, for in his greediness the rogue had swallowed them down whole. How delightful this was! So they comforted their dear mother and hopped about like tailors at a wedding.

"Now fetch some good hard stones," said the mother. "We will fill his body with them, as he lies asleep."

And so they fetched some in all haste, and put them inside him, and the mother sewed him up so quickly again that he was none the wiser.

When the wolf at last awoke, and got up, the stones inside him made him feel very thirsty, and as he was going to the brook to drink, they struck and rattled one against another. And so he cried out:

"What is this I feel inside me
Knocking hard against my bones?
How should such a thing betide me!
They were kids, and now they're stones."

So he came to the brook, and stooped to drink, but the heavy stones weighed him down, so he fell over into the water and was drowned. And when the seven little kids saw it they came up running.

"The wolf is dead, the wolf is dead!" they cried, and taking hands, they danced with their mother all about the place.

THE GOOSE GIRL

There lived once an old Queen, whose husband had been dead many years. She had a beautiful daughter who was promised in marriage to a King's son living a great way off. When the time appointed for the wedding drew near, and the old Queen had to send her daughter into the foreign land, she got together many costly things, furniture and cups and jewels and adornments, both of gold and silver, everything proper for the dowry of a royal princess, for she loved her daughter dearly. She gave her also a waiting gentlewoman to attend her and to give her into the groom's hands. And they were each to have a horse for the journey, and the Princess's horse was named Falada, and he could speak. When the time for parting came, the old Queen took her daughter to her chamber, and with a little knife she cut her own finger so that it bled. And she held beneath it a white napkin, and on it fell three drops of blood. And she gave it to her daughter, bidding her take care of it, for it would be needful to her on the way. Then they took leave of each other. And the

Princess put the napkin in her bosom, got on her horse, and set out to go to her groom. After she had ridden an hour, she began to feel very thirsty, and she said to the waiting woman,

"Get down, and fill my cup that you are carrying with water from the brook. I have great desire to drink."

"Get down yourself," said the waiting woman. "And if you are thirsty stoop down and drink. I will not be your slave."

And as her thirst was so great, the Princess had to get down and to stoop and drink of the water of the brook, and could not have her gold cup to serve her. "Oh dear!" said the poor Princess. And the three drops of blood heard her, and said,

"If your mother knew of this, it would break her heart."

But the Princess answered nothing, and quietly mounted her horse again. So they rode on some miles farther. The day was warm, the sun shone hot, and the Princess grew thirsty once more. And when they came to water she called again to the waiting woman and said,

"Get down, and give me to drink out of my golden cup." For she had forgotten all that had gone before. But the waiting woman spoke still more scornfully and said,

"If you want a drink, you may get it yourself. I am not going to be your slave."

So, as her thirst was so great, the Princess had to get off her horse and to stoop towards the running water to drink, and as she stooped, she wept and said, "Oh dear!" And the three drops of blood heard her and answered,

"If your mother knew of this, it would break her heart!"

And as she drank and stooped over, the napkin on which were the three drops of blood fell out of her bosom and floated down the stream, and in her distress she never noticed it. Not so the waiting woman, who rejoiced because she should have power over the bride, who, now that she had lost the three drops of blood, had become weak, and unable to defend herself. And when she was going to mount her horse again the waiting woman cried,

"Falada belongs to me, and this donkey to you." And the Princess had to give way and let it be as she said. Then the waiting woman ordered the Princess with many hard words to take off her rich clothing and to put on her plain garments, and then she made her swear to say nothing of the matter when they came to the royal court, threatening to take her life if she refused. And all the while Falada noticed and remembered.

The waiting woman then mounting Falada, and the Princess the sorry donkey, they journeyed on until they reached the royal castle. There was great joy at their coming, and the King's son hastened to meet them, and lifted the waiting woman from her horse, thinking she was his bride. And then he led her up the stairs, while the real Princess had to remain below. But the old King, who was looking out of the window, saw her standing in the yard, and noticed how delicate and gentle and beautiful she was, and then he went down and asked the seeming bride who it was that she had brought with her and who was now standing in the courtyard.

"Oh!" answered the bride. "I only brought her with me for

company. Give the maid something to do, that she may not be forever standing idle."

But the old King had no work to give her until he thought of a boy he had who took care of the geese, and that she might help him. And so the real Princess was sent to keep geese with the goose boy, who was called Conrad.

Soon after the false bride said to the Prince,

"Dearest husband, I pray thee do me a pleasure."

"With all my heart," answered he.

"Send for the executioner, that he may carry off the horse I came here upon, and make away with him. He was very troublesome to me on the journey." For she was afraid that the horse might tell how she had behaved to the Princess. And when the order had been given that Falada should die, it came to the Princess's ears, and she came to the executioner's man secretly, and promised him a piece of gold if he would do her a service. There was in the town a great dark gateway through which she had to pass morning and evening with her geese, and she asked the man to take Falada's head and to nail it on the gate, that she might always see it as she passed by. And the man promised, and he took Falada's head and nailed it fast in the dark gateway.

Early next morning as she and Conrad drove their geese through the gate, she said as she went by,

"O Falada, dost thou hang there?"

And the head answered,

"Princess, dost thou so meanly fare?
But if thy mother knew thy pain,
Her heart would surely break in twain."

But she went on through the town, driving her geese
to the field. And when they came into the meadows, she sat
down and undid her hair, which was all of gold, and when
Conrad saw how it glistened, he wanted to pull out a few
hairs for himself. And she said,

"O wind, blow Conrad's hat away,
Make him run after as it flies,
While I with my gold hair will play,
And twist it up in seemly wise."

Then there came a wind strong enough to blow Conrad's hat far away over the fields, and he had to run after
it. And by the time he came back she had put up her hair
with combs and pins, and he could not get at any to pull it
out. And he was sulky and would not speak to her. So they
looked after the geese until the evening came, and then they
went home.

The next morning, as they passed under the dark gateway, the Princess said,

"O Falada, dost thou hang there?"

And Falada answered,

"Princess, dost thou so meanly fare?
But if thy mother knew thy pain,
Her heart would surely break in twain."

And when they reached the fields she sat down and began to comb out her hair. Then Conrad came up and wanted to seize upon some of it, and she cried,

"O wind, blow Conrad's hat away,
Make him run after as it flies,
While I with my gold hair will play,
And do it up in seemly wise."

Then the wind came and blew Conrad's hat very far away, so that he had to run after it, and when he came back again her hair was put up again, so that he could pull none of it out. And they tended the geese until the evening.

And after they had got home, Conrad went to the old King and said, "I will tend the geese no longer with that girl!"

"Why not?" asked the old King.

"Because she vexes me the whole day long," answered Conrad. Then the old King ordered him to tell how it was.

"Every morning," said Conrad, "as we pass under the dark gateway with the geese, there is an old horse's head hanging on the wall, and she says to it,

"O Falada, dost thou hang there?"

And the head answers,

"Princess, dost thou so meanly fare?
But if thy mother knew thy pain,
Her heart would surely break in twain."

And besides this, Conrad related all that happened in the fields, and how he was obliged to run after his hat.

The old King told him to go to drive the geese next morning as usual, and he himself went behind the gate and listened how the maiden spoke to Falada. And then he followed them into the fields, and hid himself behind a bush. And he watched the goose boy and the goose girl tend the geese. And after a while he saw the girl make her hair all loose, and how it gleamed and shone. Soon she said,

"O wind, blow Conrad's hat away,
And make him follow as it flies,
While I with my gold hair will play,
And bind it up in seemly wise."

Then there came a gust of wind and away went Conrad's hat, and he after it, while the maiden combed and bound up her hair. And the old King saw all that went on. At last he went unnoticed away, and when the goose girl came back in the evening he sent for her, and asked the reason of her doing all this.

"That I dare not tell you," she answered. "Nor can I tell any man of my woe, for when I was in danger of my life I swore an oath not to reveal it." And he pressed her sore, and left her no peace, but he could get nothing out of her. At last he said,

"If you will not tell it me, tell it to the iron oven," and went away. Then she crept into the iron oven, and began to weep and to lament, and at last she opened her heart and said,

"Here I sit forsaken of all the world, and I am a King's daughter, and a wicked waiting woman forced me to give up my royal garments and my place at the bridegroom's side, and I am made a goose girl, and have to do mean service. And if my mother knew, it would break her heart."

Now the old King was standing outside by the oven door listening, and he heard all she said, and he called to her and told her to come out of the oven. And he caused royal clothing to be put upon her, and it was a marvel to see how beautiful she was. The old King then called his son and proved to him that he had the wrong bride, for she was really only a waiting woman, and that the true bride was here at hand, she who had been the goose girl. The Prince was glad at heart when he saw her beauty and gentleness. And a great feast was made ready, and all the court people and good friends were bidden to it. The groom sat in the midst with the Princess on one side and the waiting woman on the other. And the false bride did not know the true one, because she was dazzled with her glittering braveries. When all the company had eaten and drunk and were merry, the old King gave the waiting woman a question to answer, as to what such a one deserved, who had deceived her masters in such and such a manner, telling the whole story, and ending by asking,

"Now, what doom does such a one deserve?"

"No better than this," answered the false bride. "That she be put naked into a cask, studded inside with sharp nails, and be dragged along in it by two white horses from street to street, until she be dead."

"Thou hast spoken thy own doom," said the old King. "As thou hast said, so shall it be done." And when the sentence was fulfilled, the Prince married the true bride, and ever after they ruled over their Kingdom in peace and blessedness.

RAPUNZEL

There once lived a man and his wife, who had long wished for a child, but in vain. Now there was at the back of their house a little window which overlooked a beautiful garden full of the finest vegetables and flowers. But there was a high wall all round it, and no one ventured into it, for it belonged to a witch of great might, and of whom all the world was afraid. One day when the wife was standing at the window, and looking into the garden, she saw a bed filled with the finest rampion flowers. And it looked so fresh and green that she began to wish for some. And at length she longed for it greatly. This went on for days, and as she knew she could not get the rampion, she pined away, and grew pale and miserable. Then the man was uneasy, and asked,

"What is the matter, dear wife?"

"Oh," answered she. "I shall die unless I can have some of that rampion to eat that grows in the garden at the back of our house." The man, who loved her very much, thought to himself,

"Rather than lose my wife I will get some rampion, cost what it will."

So in the twilight he climbed over the wall into the witch's garden, plucked hastily a handful of rampion, and brought it to his wife. She made a salad of it at once, and ate of it to her heart's content. But she liked it so much, and it tasted so good, that the next day she longed for it thrice as much as she had done before. If she was to have any rest the man must climb over the wall once more. So he went in the twilight again. And as he was climbing back, he saw, all at once, the witch standing before him, and was terribly frightened, as she cried, with angry eyes,

"How dare you climb over into my garden like a thief, and steal my rampion! It shall be the worse for you!"

"Oh," answered he. "Be merciful rather than just, I have only done it through necessity. For my wife saw your rampion out of the window, and became possessed with so great a longing that she would have died if she could not have had some to eat." Then the witch said,

"If it is all as you say you may have as much rampion as you like, on one condition: the child that will come into the world must be given to me. It shall go well with the child, and I will care for it like a mother."

In his distress of mind the man promised everything. And when the time came when the child was born the witch appeared, and, giving the child the name of Rapunzel (which is the same as rampion), she took it away with her.

Rapunzel was the most beautiful child in the world. When she was twelve years old the witch shut her up in a tower in the midst of a wood, and it had neither steps nor door, only a small window above. When the witch wished to be let in, she would stand below and would cry,

"Rapunzel, Rapunzel! Let down your hair!"

Rapunzel had beautiful long hair that shone like gold. When she heard the voice of the witch she would undo the fastening of the upper window, unbind the plaits of her hair, and let it down twenty ells below, and the witch would climb up by it.

After they had lived thus a few years it happened that as the King's son was riding through the wood, he came to the tower. And as he drew near he heard a voice singing so sweetly that he stood still and listened. It was Rapunzel in her loneliness trying to pass away the time with sweet songs. The King's son wished to go in to her, and sought to find a door in the tower, but there was none. So he rode home, but the song had entered into his heart, and every day he went into the wood and listened to it. Once, as he was standing there under a tree, he saw the witch come up, and listened while she called out,

"O Rapunzel, Rapunzel! Let down your hair."

Then he saw how Rapunzel let down her long tresses, and how the witch climbed up by it and went in to her, and he said to himself,

"Since that is the ladder I will climb it, and seek my fortune." And the next day, as soon as it began to grow dusk, he went to the tower and cried,

"O Rapunzel, Rapunzel! Let down your hair."

And she let down her hair, and the King's son climbed up by it.

Rapunzel was greatly terrified when she saw that a man had come in to her, for she had never seen one before. But the King's son began speaking so kindly to her, and told how her singing had entered into his heart, so that he could have no peace until he had seen her herself. Then Rapunzel forgot her terror, and when he asked her to take him for her husband, and she saw that he was young and beautiful, she thought to herself,

"I certainly like him much better than old mother Gothel," and she put her hand into his hand, saying,

"I would willingly go with thee, but I do not know how I shall get out. When thou comest, bring each time a silken rope, and I will make a ladder, and when it is quite ready I will get down by it out of the tower, and thou shalt take me away on thy horse." They agreed that he should come to her every evening, as the old woman came in the day-time. So the witch knew nothing of all this until once Rapunzel said to her unwittingly,

"Mother Gothel, how is it that you climb up here so slowly, and the King's son is with me in a moment?"

"O wicked child," cried the witch. "What is this I hear! I

thought I had hidden thee from all the world, and thou hast betrayed me!"

In her anger she seized Rapunzel by her beautiful hair, struck her several times with her left hand, and then grasping a pair of shears in her right—snip, snap—the beautiful locks lay on the ground. And she was so hard-hearted that she took Rapunzel and put her in a waste and desert place, where she lived in great woe and misery.

The same day on which she took Rapunzel away she went back to the tower in the evening and made fast the severed locks of hair to the window ledge, and the King's son came and cried,

"Rapunzel, Rapunzel! Let down your hair."

Then she let the hair down, and the King's son climbed up, but instead of his dearest Rapunzel he found the witch looking at him with wicked glittering eyes.

"Aha!" cried she, mocking him. "You came for your darling, but the sweet bird sits no longer in the nest, and sings no more. The cat has got her, and will scratch out your eyes as well! Rapunzel is lost to you. You will see her no more."

The King's son was beside himself with grief, and in his agony he sprang from the tower: he escaped with life, but the thorns on which he fell put out his eyes. Then he wandered blind through the wood, eating nothing but roots and berries, and doing nothing but lament and weep for the loss of his dearest wife.

So he wandered several years in misery until at last he came to the desert place where Rapunzel lived with her twin children that she had borne, a boy and a girl. At first he heard a voice that he thought he knew, and when he reached the place from which it seemed to come Rapunzel knew him, and fell on his neck and wept. And when her tears touched his eyes they became clear again, and he could see with them as well as ever.

Then he took her to his kingdom, where he was received with great joy, and there they lived long and happily.

TOM THUMB

There was once a poor countryman who used to sit in the chimney corner all evening and poke the fire, while his wife sat at her spinning wheel.

And he used to say,

"How dull it is without any children about us. Our house is so quiet, and other people's houses so noisy and merry!"

"Yes," answered his wife, and sighed. "If we could only have one, and that one ever so little, no bigger than my thumb, how happy I should be! It would, indeed, be having our heart's desire."

Now, it happened that after a while the woman had a child who was perfect in all his limbs, but no bigger than a thumb. Then the parents said,

"He is just what we wished for, and we will love him very much," and they named him according to his stature, Tom Thumb. And though they gave him plenty of nourishment, he grew no bigger, but remained exactly the same size as when he was first born. And he had very good faculties, and was very quick and prudent, so that all he did prospered.

One day his father made ready to go into the forest to cut wood, and he said, as if to himself,

"Now, I wish there was someone to bring the cart to meet me."

"O Father," cried Tom Thumb. "I can bring the cart, let me alone for that, and in proper time, too!"

Then the father laughed, and said,

"How will you manage that? You are much too little to hold the reins."

"That has nothing to do with it, Father. While my mother goes on with her spinning I will sit in the horse's ear and tell him where to go."

"Well," answered the father, "we will try it for once."

When it was time to set off, the mother went on spinning, after setting Tom Thumb in the horse's ear. And so he drove off, crying,

"Gee-up, gee-wo!"

So the horse went on quite as if his master were driving him, and drew the wagon along the right road to the wood.

Now it happened just as they turned a corner, and the little fellow was calling out "Gee-up!," that two strange men passed by.

"Look," said one of them. "How is this? There goes a

wagon, and the driver is calling to the horse, and yet he is nowhere to be seen."

"It is very strange," said the other. "We will follow the wagon, and see where it belongs."

And the wagon went right through the wood, up to the place where the wood had been hewed. When Tom Thumb caught sight of his father, he cried out,

"Look, Father, here am I with the wagon. Now, take me down."

The father held the horse with his left hand, and with the right he lifted down his little son out of the horse's ear, and Tom Thumb sat down on a stump, quite happy and content. When the two strangers saw him they were struck dumb with wonder. At last one of them, taking the other aside, said to him, "Look here, the little chap would make our fortune if we were to show him in the town for money. Suppose we buy him."

So they went up to the woodcutter, and said,

"Sell the little man to us. We will take care he shall come to no harm."

"No," answered the father. "He is the apple of my eye, and not for all the money in the world would I sell him."

But Tom Thumb, when he heard what was going on, climbed up by his father's coattails, and, perching himself on his shoulder, he whispered in his ear,

"Father, you might as well let me go. I will soon come back again."

Then the father gave him up to the two men for a large piece of money. They asked him where he would like to sit,

"Oh, put me on the brim of your hat," said he. "There I can walk about and view the country, and be in no danger of falling off."

So they did as he wished, and when Tom Thumb had taken leave of his father, they set off all together. And they travelled on until it grew dusk, and the little fellow asked to be set down a little while for a change, and after some difficulty they consented. So the man took him down from his hat, and set him in a field by the roadside, and he ran away directly, and, after creeping about among the furrows, he slipped suddenly into a mouse hole, just what he was looking for.

"Good evening, my masters, you can go home without me!" cried he to them, laughing. They ran up and felt about with their sticks in the mouse hole, but in vain. Tom Thumb crept farther and farther in, and as it was growing dark, they had to make the best of their way home, full of vexation, and with empty purses.

When Tom Thumb found they were gone, he crept out of his hiding place underground.

"It is dangerous work groping about these holes in the darkness," said he. "I might easily break my neck."

But by good fortune he came upon an empty snail shell.

"That's all right," said he. "Now I can get safely through the night." And he settled himself down in it. Before he had time to get to sleep, he heard two men pass by, and one was saying to the other,

"How can we manage to get hold of the rich parson's gold and silver?"

"I can tell you how," cried Tom Thumb.

"How is this?" said one of the thieves, quite frightened, "I hear someone speak!"

So they stood still and listened, and Tom Thumb spoke again.

"Take me with you. I will show you how to do it!"

"Where are you, then?" asked they.

"Look about on the ground and notice where the voice comes from," answered he.

At last they found him, and lifted him up.

"You little elf," said they. "How can you help us?"

"Look here," answered he. "I can easily creep between the iron bars of the parson's room and hand out to you whatever you would like to have."

"Very well," said they. "We will try what you can do."

So when they came to the parsonage house, Tom Thumb crept into the room, but cried out with all his might,

"Will you have all that is here?" So the thieves were terrified, and said,

"Do speak more softly, lest anyone should be awaked."

But Tom Thumb made as if he did not hear them, and cried out again,

"What would you like? Will you have all that is here?" So that the cook, who was sleeping in a room hard by, heard it, and raised herself in bed and listened. The thieves, however, in their fear of being discovered, had run back part of the way, but they took courage again, thinking that it was only a jest of the little fellow's. So they came back and whispered to him to be serious, and to hand them out something.

Then Tom Thumb called out once more as loud as he could,

"Oh yes, I will give it all to you, only put out your hands."

Then the listening maid heard him distinctly that time, and jumped out of bed, and burst open the door. The thieves ran off as if the wild huntsman were behind them. But the maid, as she could see nothing, went to fetch a light. And when she came back with one, Tom Thumb had taken himself off, without being seen by her, into the barn. And the maid, when she had looked in every hole and corner and found nothing, went back to bed at last, and thought that she must have been dreaming with her eyes and ears open.

So Tom Thumb crept among the hay, and found a comfortable nook to sleep in, where he intended to remain until it was day, and then to go home to his father and mother. But other things were to befall him. Indeed, there is nothing but trouble and worry in this world! The maid got up at dawn of day to feed the cows. The first place she went to was the barn, where she took up an armful of hay, and it happened to be the very heap in which Tom Thumb lay asleep. And he was so fast asleep, that he was aware of nothing, and never waked until he was in the mouth of the cow, who had taken him up with the hay.

"Oh dear," cried he. "How is it that I have got into a mill?" But he soon found out where he was, and he had to be very careful not to get between the cow's teeth, and at last he had to descend into the cow's stomach.

"The windows were forgotten when this little room was built," said he. "And the sunshine cannot get in. There is no light to be had."

His quarters were in every way unpleasant to him, and, what was the worst, new hay was constantly coming in, and the space was being filled up. At last he cried out in his extremity, as loud as he could,

"No more hay for me! No more hay for me!"

The maid was then milking the cow, and as she heard a voice, but could see no one, and as it was the same voice that she had heard in the night, she was so frightened that she fell off her stool, and spilt the milk. Then she ran in great haste to her master, crying,

"Oh, master dear, the cow spoke!"

"You must be crazy," answered her master, and he went himself to the cow house to see what was the matter. No sooner had he put his foot inside the door, than Tom Thumb cried out again,

"No more hay for me! No more hay for me!"

Then the parson himself was frightened, supposing that a bad spirit had entered into the cow, and he ordered her to be put to death. So she was killed, but the stomach, where Tom Thumb was lying, was thrown upon a dunghill. Tom Thumb had great trouble to work his way out of it, and he had just made a space big enough for his head to go through, when a new misfortune happened. A hungry wolf ran up and swallowed the whole stomach at one gulp. But Tom Thumb did not lose courage. "Perhaps," thought he, "the wolf will listen to reason," and he cried out from the inside of the wolf,

"My dear wolf, I can tell you where to get a splendid meal!"

"Where is it to be had?" asked the wolf.

"In such and such a house, and you must creep into it through the drain, and there you will find cakes and bacon and broth, as much as you can eat," and he described to him his father's house. The wolf needed not to be told twice. He squeezed himself through the drain in the night, and feasted in the storeroom to his heart's content. When, at last, he was satisfied, he wanted to go away again, but he had become so big, that to creep the same way back was impossible. This Tom Thumb had reckoned upon, and began to make a terrible din inside the wolf, crying and calling as loud as he could.

"Will you be quiet?" said the wolf. "You will wake the folks up!"

"Look here," cried the little man. "You are very well satisfied, and now I will do something for my own enjoyment," and began again to make all the noise he could. At last the father and mother were awakened, and they ran to the room-door and peeped through the chink, and when they saw a wolf in occupation, they ran and fetched weapons—the man an axe, and the wife a scythe.

"Stay behind," said the man, as they entered the room. "When I have given him a blow, and it does not seem to have killed him, then you must cut at him with your scythe."

Then Tom Thumb heard his father's voice, and cried,

"Dear Father, I am here in the wolf's inside."

Then the father called out full of joy,

"Thank heaven that we have found our dear child!" and told his wife to keep the scythe out of the way, lest Tom Thumb should be hurt with it. Then he drew near and struck the wolf such a blow on the head that he fell down dead. And then he fetched a knife and a pair of scissors, slit up the wolf's body, and let out the little fellow.

"Oh, what anxiety we have felt about you!" said the father.

"Yes, Father, I have seen a good deal of the world, and I am very glad to breathe fresh air again."

"And where have you been all this time?" asked his father.

"Oh, I have been in a mouse hole and a snail's shell, in a

cow's stomach and a wolf's inside. Now, I think, I will stay at home."

"And we will not part with you for all the kingdoms of the world," cried the parents, as they kissed and hugged their dear little Tom Thumb. And they gave him something to eat and drink, and a new suit of clothes, as his old ones were soiled with travel.

THE TABLE, THE DONKEY, AND THE STICK

Th)here was once a tailor who had three sons and one goat. And the goat, as she nourished them all with her milk, was obliged to have good food, and so she was led every day down to the willows by the water-side. And this business the sons did in turn. One day the eldest took the goat to the churchyard, where the best sprouts are, that she might eat her fill, and gambol about.

In the evening, when it was time to go home, he said,

"Well, goat, have you had enough?"

The goat answered,

"I am so full,
I cannot pull
Another blade of grass—ba! baa!"

"Then come home," said the youth, and fastened a string to her, led her to her stall, and fastened her up.

"Now," said the old tailor, "has the goat had her proper food?"

"Oh," answered the son, "she is so full, she no more can pull."

But the father, wishing to see for himself, went out to the stall, stroked his dear goat, and said,

"My dear goat, are you full?" And the goat answered,

"How can I be full?
There was nothing to pull,
Though I looked all about me—ba! baa!"

"What is this that I hear?" cried the tailor, and he ran and called out to the youth,

"O you liar, to say that the goat was full, and she has been hungry all the time!" And in his wrath he took up his yard-measure and drove his son out of the house with many blows.

The next day came the turn of the second son, and he found a fine place in the garden hedge, where there were good green sprouts, and the goat ate them all up. In the evening, when he came to lead her home, he said,

"Well, goat, have you had enough?" And the goat answered,

"I am so full,
I could not pull
Another blade of grass—ba! baa!"

"Then come home," said the youth, and led her home, and tied her up.

"Now," said the old tailor, "has the goat had her proper food?"

"Oh," answered the son, "she is so full, she no more can pull."

The tailor, not feeling satisfied, went out to the stall, and said,

"My dear goat, are you really full?" And the goat answered,

"How can I be full?
There was nothing to pull,
Though I looked all about me—ba! baa!"

"The good-for-nothing rascal," cried the tailor, "to let the dear creature go fasting!" And, running back, he chased the youth with his yard-wand out of the house.

Then came the turn of the third son, who, meaning to make all sure, found some shrubs with the finest sprouts possible, and left the goat to devour them. In the evening, when he came to lead her home, he said,

"Well, goat, are you full?" And the goat answered,

"I am so full,
I could not pull
Another blade of grass—ba! baa!"

"Then come home," said the youth. And he took her to her stall, and fastened her up.

"Now," said the old tailor, "has the goat had her proper food?"

"Oh," answered the son, "she is so full, she no more can pull."

But the tailor, not trusting his word, went to the goat and said,

"My dear goat, are you really full?" The malicious animal answered,

"How can I be full?
There was nothing to pull,
Though I looked all about me—ba! baa!"

"Oh, the wretches!" cried the tailor. "The one as good-for-nothing and careless as the other. I will no longer have such fools about me." And rushing back, in his wrath he laid about him with his yard-wand, and belabored his son's back so unmercifully that he ran away out of the house.

So the old tailor was left alone with the goat. The next day he went out to the stall, and let out the goat, saying,

"Come, my dear creature, I will take you myself to the willows."

So he led her by the string, and brought her to the green hedges and pastures where there was plenty of food to her taste, and saying to her,

"Now, for once, you can eat to your heart's content," he left her there till the evening. Then he returned, and said,

"Well, goat, are you full?"

She answered,

"I am so full,
I could not pull
Another blade of grass—ba! baa!"

"Then come home," said the tailor, and, leading her to her stall, he fastened her up.

Before he left her he turned once more, saying,

"Now then, for once you are full." But the goat actually cried,

"How can I be full?
There was nothing to pull,
Though I looked all about me—ba! baa!"

When the tailor heard that he marveled, and saw at once that his three sons had been sent away without reason.

"Wait a minute," cried he. "You ungrateful creature! It is not enough merely to drive you away. I will teach you to show your face again among honorable tailors."

So in haste he went and fetched his razor, and seizing the goat he shaved her head as smooth as the palm of his hand. And as the yard-measure was too honorable a weapon, he took the whip and fetched her such a crack that with many a jump and spring she ran away.

The tailor felt very sad as he sat alone in his house, and would willingly have had his sons back again, but no one knew where they had gone.

The eldest son, when he was driven from home, apprenticed himself to a joiner, and he applied himself diligently to his trade, and when the time came for him to travel his master gave him a little table, nothing much to look at, and made of common wood. But it had one great quality. When anyone set it down and said, "Table, be covered!" all at once the good little table had a clean cloth on it, and a plate, and knife, and fork, and dishes with roast and boiled, and a large glass of red wine sparkling so as to cheer the heart. The young apprentice thought he was set up for life, and he went merrily out into the world, and never cared whether an inn were good or bad, or whether he could get anything to eat there or not. When he was hungry, it did not matter where he was, whether in the fields, in the woods, or in a meadow, he set down his table and said, "Be covered!" and there he was provided with everything that heart could wish. At last it occurred to him that he would go back to his father, whose wrath might by this time have subsided, and perhaps because of the wonderful table he might receive him again gladly. It happened that one evening during his journey home he came to an inn that was quite full of guests, who bade him welcome, and asked him to sit down with them and eat, as otherwise he would have found some difficulty in getting anything.

"No," answered the young joiner, "I could not think of depriving you. You had much better be my guests."

Then they laughed, and thought he must be joking. But he brought his little wooden table, and put it in the middle of the room, and said, "Table, be covered!" Immediately it was set out with food much better than the landlord had been able to provide, and the good smell of it greeted the noses of the guests very agreeably. "Fall to, good friends," said the joiner. And the guests, when they saw how it was, needed no second asking, but taking up knife and fork fell to valiantly. And what seemed most wonderful was that when a dish was empty immediately a full one stood in its place. All the while the landlord stood in a corner, and watched all that went on. He could not tell what to say about it. But he thought "such cooking as that would make my inn prosper." The joiner and his fellowship kept it up very merrily until late at night. At last they went to sleep, and the young joiner, going to bed, left his wishing table standing against the wall. The landlord, however, could not sleep for thinking of the table, and he remembered that there was in his lumber room an old table very like it, so he fetched it, and taking away the joiner's table, he left the other in its place. The next morning the joiner paid his reckoning, took up the table, not dreaming that he was carrying off the wrong one, and went on his way.

About noon he reached home, and his father received him with great joy.

"Now, my dear son, what have you learned?" said he to him.

"I have learned to be a joiner, Father," he answered.

"That is a good trade," returned the father. "But what have you brought back with you from your travels?"

"The best thing I've got, Father, is this little table," said he.

The tailor looked at it on all sides, and said,

"You have certainly produced no masterpiece. It is a rubbishing old table."

"But it is a very wonderful one," answered the son. "When I set it down, and tell it to be covered, at once the finest meats are standing on it, and wine so good that it cheers the heart. Let us invite all the friends and neighbors, that they may feast and enjoy themselves, for the table will provide enough for all."

When the company was all assembled, he put his table in the middle of the room, and said, "Table, be covered!"

But the table never stirred, and remained just as empty as any other table that does not understand talking. When the poor joiner saw that the table remained unfurnished, he felt ashamed to stand there like a fool. The company laughed at him freely, and were obliged to return unfilled and uncheered to their houses. The father gathered his pieces together and returned to his tailoring, and the son went to work under another master.

The second son had bound himself apprentice to a miller. And when his time was up, his master said to him,

"As you have behaved yourself so well, I will give you a donkey of a remarkable kind. He will draw no cart, and carry no sack."

"What is the good of him then?" asked the young apprentice.

"He spits out gold," answered the miller. "If you put a cloth before him and say, 'Bricklebrit,' out come gold pieces."

"That is a capital thing," said the apprentice, and, thanking his master, he went out into the world. Whenever he wanted gold he had only to say "Bricklebrit" to his donkey, and there was a shower of gold pieces, and so he had no cares as he travelled about. Wherever he came he lived on the best, and the dearer the better, as his purse was always full. And when he had been looking about him about the world a long time, he thought he would go and find out his father, who would perhaps forget his anger and receive him kindly because of his gold donkey. And it happened that he came to lodge in the same inn where his brother's table had been exchanged. He was leading his donkey in his hand, and the landlord was for taking the donkey from him to tie it up, but the young apprentice said,

"Don't trouble yourself, old fellow, I will take him into the stable myself and tie him up, and then I shall know where to find him."

The landlord thought this was very strange, and he never supposed that a man who was accustomed to look after his donkey himself could have much to spend. But then the stranger, feeling in his pocket, took out two gold pieces and told him to get him something good for supper. The landlord stared, and ran and fetched the best that could be got. After supper the guest called the reckoning, and the landlord, wanting to get all the profit he could, said that it would amount to two gold pieces more. The apprentice felt in his pocket, but his gold had come to an end.

"Wait a moment, landlord," said he. "I will go and fetch some money," and he went out of the room, carrying the tablecloth with him. The landlord could not tell what to make of it, and, curious to know his proceedings, slipped after him, and as the guest shut the stable door, he peeped in through a knot hole. Then he saw how the stranger spread the cloth before the donkey, saying, "Bricklebrit," and directly the donkey spat out gold, which rained upon the ground.

"Dear me," said the landlord. "That is an easy way of getting ducats. A purse of money like that is no bad thing."

After that the guest paid his reckoning and went to bed. But the landlord slipped down to the stable in the middle of the night, led the gold donkey away, and tied up another donkey in his place. The next morning early the apprentice set forth with his donkey, never doubting that it was the right one. By noon he came to his father's house, who was rejoiced to see him again, and received him gladly.

"What trade have you taken up, my son?" asked the father.

"I am a miller, dear Father," answered he.

"What have you brought home from your travels?" continued the father.

"Nothing but a donkey," answered the son.

"We have plenty of donkeys here," said the father. "You had much better have brought me a nice goat!"

"Yes," answered the son, "but this is no common donkey. When I say, 'Bricklebrit,' the good creature spits out a whole clothful of gold pieces. Let me call all the neighbors together. I will make rich people of them all."

"That will be fine!" said the tailor. "Then I need labor no more at my needle." And he rushed out himself and called the neighbors together. As soon as they were all assembled, the miller called out to them to make room, and brought in the donkey, and spread his cloth before him.

"Now, pay attention," said he, and cried, "Bricklebrit!" but no gold pieces came, and that showed that the animal was not more scientific than any other donkey.

So the poor miller made a long face when he saw that he had been taken in, and begged pardon of the neighbors, who all went home as poor as they had come. And there was nothing for it but that the old man must take to his needle again, and that the young one should take service with a miller.

The third brother had bound himself apprentice to a turner. And as turning is a very ingenious handicraft, it took him a long time to learn it. His brother told him in a letter how badly things had gone with them, and how on the last night of their travels the landlord deprived them of their treasures. When the young turner had learnt his trade, and was ready to travel, his master, to reward him for his good conduct, gave him a sack, and told him that there was a stick inside it.

"I can hang up the sack, and it may be very useful to me," said the young man. "But what is the good of the stick?"

"I will tell you," answered the master. "If any one does you any harm, and you say, 'Stick, out of the sack!' the stick will jump out upon them, and will belabor them so soundly that they shall not be able to move or to leave the place for a week, and it will not stop until you say, 'Stick, into the sack!'"

The apprentice thanked him, and took up the sack and started on his travels, and when any one attacked him he would say, "Stick, out of the sack!" and directly out jumped the stick, and dealt a shower of blows on the coat and the back beneath, which quickly ended the affair. One evening the young turner reached the inn where his two brothers had been taken in. He laid his knapsack on the table, and began to describe all the wonderful things he had seen in the world.

"Yes," said he. "You may talk of your self-spreading table,

gold-supplying donkey, and so forth. Very good things, I do not deny, but they are nothing in comparison with the treasure that I have acquired and carry with me in that sack!"

Then the landlord opened his ears.

"What in the world can it be?" thought he. "Very likely the sack is full of precious stones. And I have a perfect right to it, for all good things come in threes."

When bedtime came the guest stretched himself on a bench, and put his sack under his head for a pillow, and the landlord, when he thought the young man was sound asleep, came, and, stooping down, pulled gently at the sack, so as to remove it cautiously, and put another in its place. The turner had only been waiting for this to happen, and just as the landlord was giving a last courageous pull, he cried, "Stick, out of the sack!" Out flew the stick directly, and laid to heartily on the landlord's back. And in vain he begged for mercy. The louder he cried the harder the stick beat time on his back, until he fell exhausted to the ground. Then the turner said,

"If you do not give me the table and the donkey directly, this game shall begin all over again."

"Oh dear, no!" cried the landlord, quite collapsed. "I will gladly give it all back again if you will only make this terrible goblin go back into the sack."

Then said the young man, "I will be generous instead of just, but beware!" Then he cried, "Stick, into the sack!" and left him in peace.

The next morning the turner set out with the table and the donkey on his way home to his father. The tailor was very glad, indeed, to see him again, and asked him what he had learned abroad.

"My dear Father," answered he, "I am become a turner."

"A very ingenious handicraft," said the father. "And what have you brought with you from your travels?"

"A very valuable thing, dear Father," answered the son. "A stick in a sack!"

"What?" cried the father. "A stick! The thing is not worth so much trouble when you can cut one from any tree."

"But it is not a common stick, dear Father," said the young man. "When I say, 'Stick, out of the bag!' out jumps the stick upon any one who means harm to me, and makes him dance again, and does not leave off until he is beaten to the earth, and asks pardon. Just look here, with this stick I have recovered the table and the donkey which the thieving landlord had taken from my two brothers. Now, let them both be sent for, and bid all the neighbors too, and they shall eat and drink to their hearts' content, and I will fill their pockets with gold."

The old tailor could not quite believe in such a thing, but he called his sons and all the neighbors together. Then the turner brought in the donkey, opened a cloth before him, and said to his brother,

"Now, my dear brother, speak to him." And the miller said, "Bricklebrit!" and immediately the cloth was covered with gold pieces, until they had all got more than they could carry away. (I tell you this because it is a pity you were not there.) Then the turner set down the table, and said,

"Now, my dear brother, speak to it." And the joiner said, "Table, be covered!" and directly it was covered, and set forth plentifully with the richest dishes. Then they held a feast such as had never taken place in the tailor's house before, and the whole company remained through the night, merry and content.

The tailor after that locked up in a cupboard his needle and thread, his yard-measure and goose, and lived ever after with his three sons in great joy and splendor.

But what became of the goat, the unlucky cause of the tailor's sons being driven out? I will tell you. She felt so ashamed of her bald head that she ran into a fox's hole and hid herself. When the fox came home he caught sight of two great eyes staring at him out of the darkness, and was very frightened and ran away. A bear met him, and seeing that he looked very disturbed, asked him,

"What is the matter, brother fox, that you should look like that?"

"Oh dear," answered the fox. "A grisly beast is sitting in my hole, and he stared at me with fiery eyes!"

"We will soon drive him out," said the bear. And he went to the hole and looked in, but when he caught sight of the fiery eyes he likewise felt great terror seize him, and not wishing to have anything to do with so grisly a beast, he made off. He was soon met by a bee, who remarked that he had not a very courageous air, and said to him,

"Bear, you have a very depressed countenance, what has become of your high spirit?"

"You may well ask," answered the bear. "In the fox's hole there sits a grisly beast with fiery eyes, and we cannot drive him out."

The bee answered, "I know you despise me, bear. I am a poor feeble little creature, but I think I can help you."

So she flew into the fox's hole, and settling on the goat's smooth-shaven head, stung her so severely that she jumped up, crying, "Ba-baa!" and ran out like mad into the world. And to this hour no one knows where she ran to.

THE TWELVE BROTHERS

Once upon a time there lived a King and Queen very peacefully together. They had twelve children, all boys. Now the King said to the Queen one day,

"If our thirteenth child should be a girl the twelve boys shall die, so that her riches may be the greater, and the kingdom fall to her alone."

Then he caused twelve coffins to be made. And they were filled with shavings, and a little pillow laid in each, and they were brought and put in a locked up room. And the King gave the key to the Queen, and told her to say nothing about it to anyone.

But the mother sat the whole day sorrowing, so that her youngest son, who never left her, and to whom she had given the Bible name Benjamin, said to her,

"Dear Mother, why are you so sad?"

"Dearest child," answered she, "I dare not tell you."

But he let her have no peace until she went and unlocked

the room, and showed him the twelve coffins with the shavings and the little pillows. Then she said,

"My dear Benjamin, your father has caused these coffins to be made for you and your eleven brothers, and if I bring a little girl into the world you are all to be put to death together and buried therein." And she wept as she spoke, and her little son comforted her and said,

"Weep not, dear Mother, we will save ourselves and go far away." Then she answered,

"Yes, go with your eleven brothers out into the world, and let one of you always sit on the top of the highest tree that can be found, and keep watch upon the tower of this castle. If a little son is born I will put out a white flag, and then you may safely venture back again. But if it is a little daughter I will put out a red flag, and then flee away as fast as you can, and the dear God watch over you. Every night will I arise and pray for you. In winter that you may have a fire to warm yourselves by, and in summer that you may not languish in the heat."

After that, when she had given her sons her blessing, they went away out into the wood. One after another kept watch, sitting on the highest oak tree, looking towards the tower. When eleven days had passed, and Benjamin's turn came, he saw a flag put out, but it was not white, but blood red, to warn them that they were to die. When the brothers knew this they became angry, saying,

"Shall we suffer death because of a girl! We swear to be revenged. Wherever we find a girl we will shed her blood."

Then they went deeper into the wood. And in the middle, where it was darkest, they found a little enchanted house, standing empty. Then they said,

"Here will we dwell. And you, Benjamin, the youngest and weakest, shall stay at home and keep house. We others will go abroad and purvey food."

Then they went into the wood and caught hares, wild deer, birds, and pigeons, and whatever else is good to eat, and brought them to Benjamin for him to cook and make ready to satisfy their hunger. So they lived together in the little house for ten years, and the time did not seem long.

By this time the Queen's little daughter was growing up, she had a kind heart and a beautiful face, and a golden star on her forehead. Once when there was a great wash she saw among the clothes twelve shirts, and she asked her mother,

"Whose are these twelve shirts? They are too small to be my father's." Then the mother answered with a sore heart,

"Dear child, they belong to your twelve brothers." The little girl said,

"Where are my twelve brothers? I have never heard of them." And her mother answered,

"God only knows where they are wandering about in the world." Then she led the little girl to the secret room and unlocked it, and showed her the twelve coffins with the shavings and the little pillows.

"These coffins," said she, "were intended for your twelve brothers, but they went away far from home when you were born," and she related how everything had come to pass. Then said the little girl,

"Dear Mother, do not weep, I will go and seek my brothers."

So she took the twelve shirts and went far and wide in the great forest. The day sped on, and in the evening she came to the enchanted house. She went in and found a youth, who asked,

"Whence do you come, and what do you want?" and he marveled at her beauty, her royal garments, and the star on her forehead. Then she answered,

"I am a King's daughter, and I seek my twelve brothers, and I will go everywhere under the blue sky until I find them." And she showed him the twelve shirts which belonged to them. Then Benjamin saw that it must be his sister, and said,

"I am Benjamin, your youngest brother."

And she began weeping for joy and Benjamin also, and they kissed and cheered each other with great love. After a while he said,

"Dear sister, there is still a hindrance. We have sworn that any maiden that we meet must die, as it was because of a maiden that we had to leave our kingdom." Then she said,

"I will willingly die, if so I may benefit my twelve brothers."

"No," answered he, "you shall not die. Sit down under this tub until the eleven brothers come, and I agree with them about it." She did so. And as night came on they returned from hunting, and supper was ready. And as they were sitting at table and eating, they asked,

"What news?" And Benjamin said,

"Don't you know any?"

"No," answered they. So he said,

"You have been in the wood, and I have stayed at home, and yet I know more than you."

"Tell us!" cried they. He answered,

"Promise me that the first maiden we see shall not be put to death."

"Yes, we promise," cried they all. "She shall have mercy. Tell us now." Then he said,

"Our sister is here," and lifted up the tub, and the King's daughter came forth in her royal garments with her golden star on her forehead, and she seemed so beautiful, delicate, and sweet, that they all rejoiced, and fell on her neck and kissed her, and loved her with all their hearts.

After this she remained with Benjamin in the house and helped him with the work. The others went forth into the woods to catch wild animals, does, birds, and pigeons, for food for them all, and their sister and Benjamin took care that all was made ready for them. She fetched the wood for cooking, and the vegetables, and watched the pots on the fire, so that supper was always ready when the others came in. She kept also great order in the house, and the beds were always beautifully white and clean, and the brothers were contented, and lived in unity.

One day the two got ready a fine feast, and when they were all assembled they sat down and ate and drank, and were full of joy. Now there was a little garden belonging to the enchanted house, in which grew twelve lilies. The maiden, thinking to please her brothers, went out to gather the twelve flowers, meaning to give one to each as they sat at meat. But as she broke off the flowers, in the same moment the brothers were changed into twelve ravens, and flew over the wood far away, and the house with the garden also disappeared. So the poor maiden stood alone in the wild wood, and as she was looking around her she saw an old woman standing by her, who said,

"My child, what hast thou done? Why couldst thou not leave the twelve flowers standing? They were thy twelve brothers, who are now changed to ravens forever." The maiden said, weeping,

"Is there no means of setting them free?"

"No," said the old woman. "There is in the whole world no way but one, and that is difficult. Thou canst not release them but by being dumb for seven years. Thou must neither speak nor laugh. And wert thou to speak one single word, and it wanted but one hour of the seven years, all would be in vain, and thy brothers would perish because of that one word."

Then the maiden said in her heart, "I am quite sure that I can set my brothers free," and went and sought a tall tree, climbed up, and sat there spinning, and never spoke or laughed. Now it happened that a King, who was hunting in the wood, had with him a large greyhound, who ran to the tree where the maiden was, sprang up at it, and barked loudly. Up came the King and saw the beautiful Princess with the golden star on her forehead, and he was so charmed with her beauty that he prayed her to become his wife. She gave no answer, only a little nod of her head. Then he himself climbed the tree and brought her down, set her on his horse, and took her home. The wedding was held with great splendor and rejoicing, but the bride neither spoke nor laughed. After they had lived pleasantly together for a few years, the King's mother, who was a wicked woman, began to slander the young Queen, and said to the King,

"She is only a low beggar maid that you have taken to yourself. Who knows what mean tricks she is playing? Even if she is really dumb and cannot speak she might at least laugh. Not to laugh is the sign of a bad conscience."

At first the King would believe nothing of it, but the old woman talked so long, and suggested so many bad things, that he at last let himself be persuaded, and condemned the Queen to death.

Now a great fire was kindled in the courtyard, and she was to be burned in it. And the King stood above at the window, and watched it all with weeping eyes, for he had held her very dear. And when she was already fast bound to the stake, and the fire was licking her garments with red tongues, the last moment of the seven years came to an end. Then a rushing sound was heard in the air, and twelve ravens came flying and sank downwards. And as they touched the earth they became her twelve brothers that she had lost. They rushed through the fire and quenched the flames, and set their dear sister free, kissing and consoling her. And now that her mouth was opened, and that she might venture to speak, she told the King the reason of her dumbness, and why she had never laughed. The King rejoiced when he heard of her innocence, and they all lived together in happiness until their death.

But the wicked mother-in-law was very unhappy, and died miserably.

THE FISHERMAN AND HIS WIFE

There was once a fisherman and his wife who lived together in a hovel by the seashore, and the fisherman went out every day with his hook and line to catch fish, and he angled and angled.

One day he was sitting with his rod and looking into the clear water, and he sat and sat.

At last down went the line to the bottom of the water, and when he drew it up he found a great flounder on the hook. And the flounder said to him,

"Fisherman, listen to me. Let me go, I am not a real fish but an enchanted prince. What good shall I be to you if you land me? I shall not taste well. So put me back into the water again, and let me swim away."

"Well," said the fisherman. "No need of so many words about the matter, as you can speak I had much rather let you swim away."

Then he put him back into the clear water, and the flounder sank to the bottom, leaving a long streak of blood behind him. Then the fisherman got up and went home to his wife in their hovel.

"Well, husband," said the wife, "have you caught nothing today?"

"No," said the man. "That is, I did catch a flounder, but as he said he was an enchanted prince, I let him go again."

"Then, did you wish for nothing?" said the wife.

"No," said the man. "What should I wish for?"

"Oh dear!" said the wife. "And it is so dreadful always to live in this evil-smelling hovel. You might as well have wished for a little cottage. Go again and call him. Tell him we want a little cottage, I daresay he will give it us. Go, and be quick."

And when he went back, the sea was green and yellow, and not nearly so clear. So he stood and said,

"O man, O man!—if man you be,
Or flounder, flounder, in the sea—
Such a tiresome wife I've got,
For she wants what I do not."

Then the flounder came swimming up, and said,
"Now then, what does she want?"

"Oh," said the man. "You know when I caught you my wife says I ought to have wished for something. She does not want to live any longer in the hovel, and would rather have a cottage."

"Go home with you," said the flounder. "She has it already."

So the man went home, and found, instead of the hovel, a little cottage, and his wife was sitting on a bench before the door. And she took him by the hand, and said to him,

"Come in and see if this is not a great improvement."

So they went in, and there was a little common place and a beautiful little bedroom, a kitchen and larder, with all sorts of furniture, and iron and brass ware of the very best. And at the back was a little yard with fowls and ducks, and a little garden full of green vegetables and fruit.

"Look," said the wife, "is not that nice?"

"Yes," said the man. "If this can only last we shall be very well contented."

"We will see about that," said the wife. And after a meal they went to bed.

So all went well for a week or fortnight, when the wife said,

"Look here, husband, the cottage is really too confined, and the yard and garden are so small. I think the flounder had better get us a larger house. I should like very much to live in a large stone castle. So go to your fish and he will send us a castle."

"O my dear wife," said the man, "the cottage is good enough. What do we want a castle for?"

"We want one," said the wife. "Go along with you. The flounder can give us one."

"Now, wife," said the man, "the flounder gave us the cottage. I do not like to go to him again, he may be angry."

"Go along," said the wife, "he might just as well give us it as not. Do as I say!"

The man felt very reluctant and unwilling. And he said to himself,

"It is not the right thing to do." Nevertheless he went.

So when he came to the seaside, the water was purple and dark blue and gray and thick, and not green and yellow as before. And he stood and said,

"O man, O man!—if man you be,
Or flounder, flounder, in the sea—
Such a tiresome wife I've got,
For she wants what I do not."

"Now then, what does she want?" said the flounder.

"Oh," said the man, half frightened, "she wants to live in a large stone castle."

"Go home with you, she is already standing before the door," said the flounder.

Then the man went home, as he supposed, but when he got there, there stood in the place of the cottage a great castle of stone, and his wife was standing on the steps, about to go in. So she took him by the hand, and said,

"Let us enter."

With that he went in with her, and in the castle was a great hall with a marble pavement, and there were a great many servants, who led them through large doors, and the passages were decked with tapestry, and the rooms with golden chairs and tables, and crystal chandeliers hanging from the ceiling. And all the rooms had carpets. And the tables were covered with eatables and the best wine for anyone who wanted them. And at the back of the house was a great stable yard for horses and cattle, and the finest carriages. Besides, there was a splendid large garden, with the most beautiful flowers and fine fruit trees, and a pleasance full half a mile long, with deer and oxen and sheep, and everything that heart could wish for.

"There!" said the wife. "Is this not beautiful?"

"Oh yes," said the man. "If it will only last we can live in this fine castle and be very well contented."

"We will see about that," said the wife. "In the meanwhile we will sleep upon it." With that they went to bed.

The next morning the wife was awake first, just at the break of day, and she looked out and saw from her bed the beautiful country lying all around. The man took no notice of it, so she poked him in the side with her elbow, and said,

"Husband, get up and just look out of the window. Look, just think if we could be King over all this country. Just go to your fish and tell him we should like to be King."

"Now, wife," said the man, "what should we be Kings for? I don't want to be King."

"Well," said the wife, "if you don't want to be King, I will be King."

"Now, wife," said the man, "what do you want to be King for? I could not ask him such a thing."

"Why not?" said the wife. "You must go directly all the same. I must be King."

So the man went, very much put out that his wife should want to be King.

"It is not the right thing to do. Not at all the right thing," thought the man. He did not at all want to go, and yet he went all the same.

And when he came to the sea the water was quite dark gray, and rushed far inland, and had an ill smell. And he stood and said,

"O man, O man!—if man you be,
Or flounder, flounder, in the sea—
Such a tiresome wife I've got,
For she wants what I do not."

"Now then, what does she want?" said the fish.

"Oh dear!" said the man. "She wants to be King."

"Go home with you, she is so already," said the fish.

So the man went back, and as he came to the palace he saw it was very much larger, and had great towers and splendid gateways. The herald stood before the door, and a number of soldiers with kettle-drums and trumpets.

And when he came inside everything was of marble and gold, and there were many curtains with great golden tassels. Then he went through the doors of the saloon to where the great throne room was, and there was his wife sitting upon a throne of gold and diamonds, and she had a great golden crown on, and the scepter in her hand was of pure gold and jewels, and on each side stood six pages in a row, each one a head shorter than the other. So the man went up to her and said,

"Well, wife, so now you are King!"

"Yes," said the wife, "now I am King."

So then he stood and looked at her, and when he had gazed at her for some time he said,

"Well, wife, this is fine for you to be King! Now there is nothing more to wish for."

"O husband!" said the wife, seeming quite restless. "I am tired of this already. Go to your fish and tell him that now I am King I must be emperor."

"Now, wife," said the man. "What do you want to be emperor for?"

"Husband," said she, "go and tell the fish I want to be emperor."

"Oh dear!" said the man. "He could not do it. I cannot ask him such a thing. There is but one emperor at a time. The fish can't possibly make anyone emperor, indeed he can't."

"Now, look here," said the wife. "I am King, and you are only my husband, so will you go at once? Go along! For if he was able to make me king he is able to make me emperor. And I will and must be emperor, so go along!"

So he was obliged to go. And as he went he felt very uncomfortable about it, and he thought to himself,

"It is not at all the right thing to do. To want to be emperor is really going too far. The flounder will soon be beginning to get tired of this."

With that he came to the sea, and the water was quite black and thick, and the foam flew, and the wind blew, and the man was terrified. But he stood and said,

"O man, O man!—if man you be,
Or flounder, flounder, in the sea—
Such a tiresome wife I've got,
For she wants what I do not."

"What is it now?" said the fish.

"Oh dear!" said the man. "My wife wants to be emperor."

"Go home with you," said the fish. "She is emperor already."

So the man went home, and found the castle adorned with polished marble and alabaster figures, and golden gates. The troops were being marshaled before the door, and they were blowing trumpets and beating drums and cymbals. And when he entered he saw barons and earls and dukes waiting about like servants. And the doors were of bright gold.

And he saw his wife sitting upon a throne made of one entire piece of gold, and it was about two miles high. And she had a great golden crown on, which was about three yards high, set with brilliants and carbuncles. And in one hand she held the scepter, and in the other the globe. And on both sides of her stood pages in two rows, all arranged according to their size, from the most enormous giant of two miles high to the tiniest dwarf of the size of my little finger. And before her stood earls and dukes in crowds. So the man went up to her and said,

"Well, wife, so now you are emperor."

"Yes," said she, "now I am emperor."

Then he went and sat down and had a good look at her, and then he said,

"Well now, wife, there is nothing left to be, now that you are emperor."

"What are you talking about, husband?" said she. "I am emperor, and next I will be pope! So go and tell the fish so."

"Oh dear!" said the man. "What is it that you don't want? You can never become pope. There is but one pope in Christendom, and the fish can't possibly do it."

"Husband," said she, "no more words about it. I must and will be pope. So go along to the fish."

"Now, wife," said the man, "how can I ask him such a thing? It is too bad. It is asking a little too much. And, besides, he could not do it."

"What rubbish!" said the wife. "If he could make me emperor he can make me pope. Go along and ask him. I am emperor, and you are only my husband, so go you must."

So he went, feeling very frightened, and he shivered and shook, and his knees trembled. And there arose a great wind, and the clouds flew by, and it grew very dark, and the sea rose mountains high, and the ships were tossed about, and the sky was partly blue in the middle, but at the sides very dark and red, as in a great tempest. And he felt very desponding, and stood trembling and said,

> "O man, O man!—if man you be,
> Or flounder, flounder, in the sea—
> Such a tiresome wife I've got,
> For she wants what I do not."

"Well, what now?" said the fish.

"Oh dear!" said the man. "She wants to be pope."

"Go home with you, she is pope already," said the fish.

So he went home, and he found himself before a great church, with palaces all round. He had to make his way through a crowd of people. And when he got inside he found the place lighted up with thousands and thousands of lights. And his wife was clothed in a golden garment, and sat upon a very high throne, and had three golden crowns on, all in the greatest priestly pomp. And on both sides of her there stood two rows of lights of all sizes, from the size of the longest tower to the smallest candle, and all the emperors and Kings were kneeling before her and kissing her foot.

"Well, wife," said the man, and sat and stared at her, "so you are pope."

"Yes," said she, "now I am pope!"

And he went on gazing at her till he felt dazzled, as if he were sitting in the sun. And after a little time he said,

"Well, now, wife, what is there left to be, now you are pope?"

And she sat up very stiff and straight, and said nothing.

And he said again, "Well, wife, I hope you are contented at last with being pope. You can be nothing more."

"We will see about that," said the wife. With that they both went to bed. But she was as far as ever from being contented, and she could not get to sleep for thinking of what she should like to be next.

The husband, however, slept as fast as a top after his busy day. But the wife tossed and turned from side to side the whole night through, thinking all the while what she could be next, but nothing would occur to her. And when she saw the red dawn she slipped off the bed, and sat before the window to see the sun rise, and as it came up she said,

"Ah, I have it! What if I should make the sun and moon to rise—husband!" she cried, and stuck her elbow in his ribs. "Wake up, and go to your fish, and tell him I want power over the sun and moon."

The man was so fast asleep that when he started up he fell out of bed. Then he shook himself together, and opened his eyes and said,

"Oh—wife, what did you say?"

"Husband," said she, "if I cannot get the power of making the sun and moon rise when I want them, I shall never have another quiet hour. Go to the fish and tell him so."

"O wife!" said the man, and fell on his knees to her. "The fish can really not do that for you. I grant you he could make you emperor and pope. Do be contented with that, I beg of you."

And she became wild with impatience, and screamed out,

"I can wait no longer, go at once!"

And so off he went as well as he could for fright. And a dreadful storm arose, so that he could hardly keep his feet. And the houses and trees were blown down, and the mountains trembled, and rocks fell in the sea. The sky was quite black, and it thundered and lightened. And the waves, crowned with foam, ran mountains high. So he cried out, without being able to hear his own words,

"O man, O man!—if man you be,
Or flounder, flounder, in the sea—
Such a tiresome wife I've got,
For she wants what I do not."

"Well, what now?" said the flounder.

"Oh dear!" said the man. "She wants to order about the sun and moon."

"Go home with you!" said the flounder. "You will find her in the old hovel."

And there they are sitting to this very day.

LITTLE RED CAP

There was once a sweet little maid, much beloved by everybody, but most of all by her grandmother, who never knew how to make enough of her. Once she sent her a little cap of red velvet, and as it was very becoming to her, and she never wore anything else, people called her Little Red Cap. One day her mother said to her,

"Come, Little Red Cap, here are some cakes and a flask of wine for you to take to Grandmother. She is weak and ill, and they will do her good. Make haste and start before it grows hot, and walk properly and nicely, and don't run, or you might fall and break the flask of wine, and there would be none left for Grandmother. And when you go into her room, don't forget to say good morning, instead of staring about you."

"I will be sure to take care," said Little Red Cap to her mother, and gave her hand upon it. Now the grandmother lived away in the wood, half-an-hour's walk from the village. And when Little Red Cap had reached the wood, she met the wolf. But as she did not know what a bad sort of animal he was, she did not feel frightened.

"Good day, Little Red Cap," said he.

"Thank you kindly, Wolf," answered she.

"Where are you going so early, Little Red Cap?"

"To my grandmother's."

"What are you carrying under your apron?"

"Cakes and wine. We baked yesterday. And my grandmother is very weak and ill, so they will do her good, and strengthen her."

"Where does your grandmother live, Little Red Cap?"

"A quarter of an hour's walk from here. Her house stands beneath the three oak trees, and you may know it by the hazel bushes," said Little Red Cap. The wolf thought to himself,

"That tender young thing would be a delicious morsel, and would taste better than the old one. I must manage somehow to get both of them."

Then he walked by Little Red Cap a little while, and said,

"Little Red Cap, just look at the pretty flowers that are growing all round you, and I don't think you are listening to the song of the birds. You are posting along just as if you were going to school, and it is so delightful out here in the wood."

Little Red Cap glanced round her, and when she saw the sunbeams darting here and there through the trees, and lovely flowers everywhere, she thought to herself,

"If I were to take a fresh nosegay to my grandmother

she would be very pleased, and it is so early in the day that I shall reach her in plenty of time." And so she ran about in the wood, looking for flowers. And as she picked one she saw a still prettier one a little farther off, and so she went farther and farther into the wood. But the wolf went straight to the grandmother's house and knocked at the door.

"Who is there?" cried the grandmother.

"Little Red Cap," he answered. "I have brought you some cake and wine. Please open the door."

"Lift the latch," cried the grandmother. "I am too feeble to get up."

So the wolf lifted the latch, and the door flew open, and he fell on the grandmother and ate her up without saying one word. Then he drew on her clothes, put on her cap, lay down in her bed, and drew the curtains.

Little Red Cap was all this time running about among the flowers, and when she had gathered as many as she could hold, she remembered her grandmother, and set off to go to her. She was surprised to find the door standing open, and when she came inside she felt very strange, and thought to herself,

"Oh dear, how uncomfortable I feel, and I was so glad this morning to go to my grandmother!"

And when she said, "Good morning," there was no answer. Then she went up to the bed and drew back the curtains. There lay the grandmother with her cap pulled over her eyes, so that she looked very odd.

"O Grandmother, what large ears you have got!"

"The better to hear with."

"O Grandmother, what great eyes you have got!"

"The better to see with."

"O Grandmother, what large hands you have got!"

"The better to take hold of you with."

"But, Grandmother, what a terrible large mouth you have got!"

"The better to devour you!" And no sooner had the wolf said it than he made one bound from the bed, and swallowed up poor Little Red Cap.

Then the wolf, having satisfied his hunger, lay down again in the bed, went to sleep, and began to snore loudly. The huntsman heard him as he was passing by the house, and thought,

"How the old woman snores! I had better see if there is anything the matter with her."

Then he went into the room, and walked up to the bed and saw the wolf lying there.

"At last I find you, you old sinner!" said he. "I have been looking for you a long time." And he made up his mind that the wolf had swallowed the grandmother whole, and that she might yet be saved. So he did not fire, but took a pair of shears and began to slit up the wolf's body. When he made a few snips Little Red Cap appeared, and after a few more snips she jumped out and cried, "Oh dear, how frightened I have been! It is so dark inside the wolf." And then out came the old grandmother, still living and breathing. But Little Red Cap went and quickly fetched some large stones, with which she filled the wolf's body, so that when he woke up, and was going to rush away, the stones were so heavy that he sank down and fell dead.

They were all three very pleased. The huntsman took off the wolf's skin, and carried it home. The grandmother ate the cakes, and drank the wine, and held up her head again, and Little Red Cap said to herself that she would never more stray about in the wood alone, but would mind what her mother told her.

It must also be related how a few days afterwards, when Little Red Cap was again taking cakes to her grandmother, another wolf spoke to her, and wanted to tempt her to leave the path. But she was on her guard, and went straight on her way, and told her grandmother how the wolf had met her, and wished her good day, but had looked so wicked about the eyes that she thought if it had not been on the high road he would have devoured her.

"Come," said the grandmother. "We will shut the door, so that he may not get in."

Soon after came the wolf knocking at the door, and calling out, "Open the door, Grandmother, I am Little Red Cap, bringing you cakes." But they remained still, and did not open the door. After that the wolf slunk by the house, and got at last upon the roof to wait until Little Red Cap should return home in the evening. Then he meant to spring down upon her, and devour her in the darkness. But the grandmother discovered his plot. Now there stood before the house a great stone trough, and the grandmother said to the child, "Little Red Cap, I was boiling sausages yesterday, so take the bucket, and carry away the water they were boiled in, and pour it into the trough."

And Little Red Cap did so until the great trough was quite full. When the smell of the sausages reached the nose of the wolf he snuffed it up, and looked round, and stretched out his neck so far that he lost his balance and began to slip, and he slipped down off the roof straight into the great trough, and was drowned. Then Little Red Cap went cheerfully home, and came to no harm.

THE ALMOND TREE

A long time ago, perhaps as much as two thousand years, there was a rich man, and he had a beautiful and pious wife, and they loved each other very much, and they had no children, though they wished greatly for some, and the wife prayed for one day and night. Now, in the courtyard in front of their house stood an almond tree. And one day in winter the wife was standing beneath it, and paring an apple, and as she pared it she cut her finger, and the blood fell upon the snow.

"Ah," said the woman, sighing deeply, and looking down at the blood. "If only I could have a child as red as blood, and as white as snow!"

And as she said these words, her heart suddenly grew light, and she felt sure she should have her wish. So she went back to the house, and when a month had passed the snow was gone. In two months everything was green. In three months the flowers sprang out of the earth. In four months the trees were in full leaf, and the branches were thickly entwined. The little birds began to sing, so that the woods echoed, and the blossoms fell from the trees. When the fifth month had passed the wife stood under the almond tree, and it smelt so sweet that her heart leaped within her, and she fell on her knees for joy. And when the sixth month had gone, the fruit was thick and fine, and she remained still. And the seventh month she gathered the almonds, and ate them eagerly, and was sick and sorrowful. And when the eighth month had passed she called to her husband, and said, weeping,

"If I die, bury me under the almond tree."

Then she was comforted and happy until the ninth month had passed, and then she bore a child as white as snow and as red as blood, and when she saw it her joy was so great that she died.

Her husband buried her under the almond tree, and he wept sore. Time passed, and he became less sad. And after he had grieved a little more he left off, and then he took another wife.

His second wife bore him a daughter, and his first wife's child was a son, as red as blood and as white as snow. Whenever the wife looked at her daughter she felt great love for her, but whenever she looked at the little boy, evil thoughts came into her heart, of how she could get all her husband's money for her daughter, and how the boy stood in the way. And so she took great hatred to him, and drove him from one corner to another, and gave him a buffet here and a cuff there, so that the poor child was always in disgrace. When he came back after school hours there was no peace for him.

Once, when the wife went into the room upstairs, her little daughter followed her, and said,

"Mother, give me an apple."

"Yes, my child," said the mother, and gave her a fine apple out of the chest, and the chest had a great heavy lid with a strong iron lock.

"Mother," said the little girl, "shall not my brother have one too?"

That was what the mother expected, and she said,

"Yes, when he comes back from school."

And when she saw from the window that he was coming, an evil thought crossed her mind, and she snatched the apple, and took it from her little daughter, saying,

"You shall not have it before your brother."

Then she threw the apple into the chest, and shut to the lid. Then the little boy came in at the door, and she said to him in a kind tone, but with evil looks,

"My son, will you have an apple?"

"Mother," said the boy, "how terrible you look! Yes, give me an apple!"

Then she spoke as kindly as before, holding up the cover of the chest,

"Come here and take out one for yourself."

And as the boy was stooping over the open chest, crash

went the lid down, so that his head flew off among the red apples. But then the woman felt great terror, and wondered how she could escape the blame. And she went to the chest of drawers in her bedroom and took a white handkerchief out of the nearest drawer, and fitting the head to the neck, she bound them with the handkerchief, so that nothing should be seen, and set him on a chair before the door with the apple in his hand.

Then came little Marjory into the kitchen to her mother, who was standing before the fire stirring a pot of hot water.

"Mother," said Marjory, "my brother is sitting before the door and he has an apple in his hand, and looks very pale. I asked him to give me the apple, but he did not answer me. It seems very strange."

"Go again to him," said the mother. "And if he will not answer you, give him a box on the ear."

So Marjory went again and said,

"Brother, give me the apple."

But as he took no notice, she gave him a box on the ear, and his head fell off, at which she was greatly terrified, and began to cry and scream, and ran to her mother, and said,

"O Mother! I have knocked my brother's head off!" and cried and screamed, and would not cease.

"O Marjory!" said her mother. "What have you done? But keep quiet, that no one may see there is anything the matter. It can't be helped now. We will put him out of the way safely."

When the father came home and sat down to table, he said,

"Where is my son?"

But the mother was filling a great dish full of black broth, and Marjory was crying bitterly, for she could not refrain. Then the father said again,

"Where is my son?"

"Oh," said the mother. "He is gone into the country to his great uncle's to stay for a little while."

"What should he go for?" said the father. "And without bidding me good-bye, too!"

"Oh, he wanted to go so much, and he asked me to let him stay there six weeks. He will be well taken care of."

"Dear me," said the father. "I am quite sad about it. It was not right of him to go without bidding me good-bye."

With that he began to eat, saying,

"Marjory, what are you crying for? Your brother will come back some time."

After a while he said,

"Well, wife, the food is very good. Give me some more."

And the more he ate the more he wanted, until he had eaten it all up, and he threw the bones under the table. Then Marjory went to her chest of drawers, and took one of her best handkerchiefs from the bottom drawer, and picked up all the bones from under the table and tied them up in her hand-kerchief, and went out at the door crying bitterly. She laid them in the green grass under the almond tree, and immediately her heart grew light again, and she wept no more. Then the almond tree began to wave to and fro, and the boughs drew together and then parted, just like a clapping of hands for joy. Then a cloud rose from the tree, and in the midst of the cloud there burned a fire, and out of the fire a beautiful bird arose, and, singing most sweetly, soared high into the air. And when he had flown away, the almond tree remained as it was before, but the handkerchief full of bones was gone. Marjory felt quite glad and light-hearted, just as if her brother were still alive. So she went back merrily into the house and had her dinner.

The bird, when it flew away, perched on the roof of a goldsmith's house, and began to sing,

"It was my mother who murdered me.
It was my father who ate of me.
It was my sister Marjory
Who all my bones in pieces found.
Them in a handkerchief she bound,
And laid them under the almond tree.
Kywitt, kywitt, kywitt, I cry,
Oh what a beautiful bird am I!"

The goldsmith was sitting in his shop making a golden chain, and when he heard the bird, who was sitting on his roof and singing, he started up to go and look, and as he passed over his threshold he lost one of his slippers. And he went into the middle of the street with a slipper on one foot and only a sock on the other, with his apron on, and the gold chain in one hand and the pincers in the other. And so he stood in the sunshine looking up at the bird.

"Bird," said he, "how beautifully you sing. Do sing that piece over again."

"No," said the bird. "I do not sing for nothing twice. If you will give me that gold chain I will sing again."

"Very well," said the goldsmith. "Here is the gold chain. Now do as you said."

Down came the bird and took the gold chain in his right claw, perched in front of the goldsmith, and sang,

"It was my mother who murdered me.
It was my father who ate of me.
It was my sister Marjory
Who all my bones in pieces found.
Them in a handkerchief she bound,
And laid them under the almond tree.
Kywitt, kywitt, kywitt, I cry,
Oh what a beautiful bird am I!"

Then the bird flew to a shoemaker's, and perched on his roof, and sang,

"It was my mother who murdered me.
It was my father who ate of me.
It was my sister Marjory
Who all my bones in pieces found.
Them in a handkerchief she bound,
And laid them under the almond tree.
Kywitt, kywitt, kywitt, I cry,
Oh what a beautiful bird am I!"

When the shoemaker heard, he ran out of his door in his shirt sleeves and looked up at the roof of his house, holding his hand to shade his eyes from the sun.

"Bird," said he, "how beautifully you sing!"

Then he called in at his door,

"Wife, come out directly. Here is a bird singing beautifully. Only listen."

Then he called his daughter, all his children, and acquaintance, both young men and maidens, and they came up the street and gazed on the bird, and saw how beautiful it was with red and green feathers, and round its throat was as it were gold, and its eyes twinkled in its head like stars.

"Bird," said the shoemaker, "do sing that piece over again."

"No," said the bird. "I may not sing for nothing twice. You must give me something."

"Wife," said the man, "go into the shop. On the top shelf stands a pair of red shoes. Bring them here."

So the wife went and brought the shoes.

"Now bird," said the man, "sing us that piece again."

And the bird came down and took the shoes in his left claw, and flew up again to the roof, and sang,

"It was my mother who murdered me.
It was my father who ate of me.
It was my sister Marjory
Who all my bones in pieces found.
Them in a handkerchief she bound,
And laid them under the almond tree.
Kywitt, kywitt, kywitt, I cry,
Oh what a beautiful bird am I!"

And when he had finished he flew away, with the chain in his right claw and the shoes in his left claw, and he flew till he reached a mill, and the mill went "clip-clap, clip-clap, clip-clap." And in the mill sat twenty millers men hewing a millstone—"hick-hack, hick-hack, hick-hack," while the mill was going "clip-clap, clip-clap, clip-clap." And the bird perched on a linden tree that stood in front of the mill, and sang,

"It was my mother who murdered me."

Here one of the men looked up.

"It was my father who ate of me."

Then two more looked up and listened.

"It was my sister Marjory"

Here four more looked up.

"Who all my bones in pieces found.
Them in a handkerchief she bound,"

Now there were only eight left hewing.

"And laid them under the almond tree."

Now only five.

"Kywitt, kywitt, kywitt, I cry,"

Now only one.

"Oh what a beautiful bird am I!"

At length the last one left off, and he only heard the end.
"Bird," said he, "how beautifully you sing. Let me hear it all. Sing that again!"

"No," said the bird. "I may not sing it twice for nothing. If you will give me the millstone I will sing it again."

"Indeed," said the man. "If it belonged to me alone you should have it."

"All right," said the others. "If he sings again he shall have it."

Then the bird came down, and all the twenty millers heaved up the stone with poles, "yo! heave-ho! yo! heave-ho!" and the bird stuck his head through the hole in the middle, and with the millstone round his neck he flew up to the tree and sang,

"It was my mother who murdered me.
It was my father who ate of me.
It was my sister Marjory
Who all my bones in pieces found.
Them in a handkerchief she bound,
And laid them under the almond tree.
Kywitt, kywitt, kywitt, I cry,
Oh what a beautiful bird am I!"

And when he had finished, he spread his wings, having in the right claw the chain, and in the left claw the shoes, and round his neck the millstone, and he flew away to his father's house.

In the parlor sat the father, the mother, and Marjory at the table. The father said,

"How light-hearted and cheerful I feel."

"Nay," said the mother. "I feel very low, just as if a great storm were coming."

But Marjory sat weeping. And the bird came flying, and perched on the roof.

"Oh," said the father. "I feel so joyful, and the sun is shining so bright. It is as if I were going to meet with an old friend."

"Nay," said the wife. "I am terrified, my teeth chatter, and there is fire in my veins," and she tore open her dress to get air. And Marjory sat in a corner and wept, with her plate before her, until it was quite full of tears. Then the bird perched on the almond tree, and sang,

"It was my mother who murdered me."

And the mother stopped her ears and hid her eyes, and would neither see nor hear. Nevertheless, the noise of a fearful storm was in her ears, and in her eyes a quivering and burning as of lightning.

"It was my father who ate of me."

"O Mother!" said the father. "There is a beautiful bird singing so finely, and the sun shines, and everything smells as sweet as cinnamon."

"It was my sister Marjory"

Marjory hid her face in her lap and wept, and the father said,

"I must go out to see the bird."

"Oh do not go!" said the wife. "I feel as if the house were on fire."

But the man went out and looked at the bird.

Who all my bones in pieces found.
Them in a handkerchief she bound,
And laid them under the almond tree.
Kywitt, kywitt, kywitt, I cry,
Oh what a beautiful bird am I!"

With that the bird let fall the gold chain upon his father's neck, and it fitted him exactly. So he went indoors and said,

"Look what a beautiful chain the bird has given me."

Then his wife was so terrified that she fell all along on the floor, and her cap came off. Then the bird began again to sing,

"It was my mother who murdered me."

"Oh," groaned the mother. "That I were a thousand fathoms underground, so as not to be obliged to hear it."

"It was my father who ate of me."

Then the woman lay as if she were dead.

"It was my sister Marjory"

"Oh," said Marjory. "I will go out, too, and see if the bird will give me anything." And so she went.

"Who all my bones in pieces found.
Them in a handkerchief she bound,"

Then he threw the shoes down to her.

And laid them under the almond tree.
Kywitt, kywitt, kywitt, I cry,
Oh what a beautiful bird am I!"

And poor Marjory all at once felt happy and joyful, and put on her red shoes, and danced and jumped for joy.

"Oh dear," said she. "I felt so sad before I went outside, and now my heart is so light! He is a charming bird to have given me a pair of red shoes."

But the mother's hair stood on end, and looked like flame, and she said,

"Even if the world is coming to an end, I must go out for a little relief."

Just as she came outside the door, crash went the millstone on her head, and crushed her flat. The father and daughter rushed out, and saw smoke and flames of fire rise up. But when that had gone by, there stood the little brother. And he took his father and Marjory by the hand, and they felt very happy and content, and went indoors, and sat to the table, and had their dinner.

PRUDENT HANS

One day, Hans's mother said,

"Where are you going, Hans?" Hans answered,

"To Grethel's, Mother."

"Manage well, Hans."

"All right! Good-bye, Mother."

"Good-bye, Hans."

Then Hans came to Grethel's.

"Good morning, Grethel."

"Good morning, Hans. What have you brought me today?"

"I have brought nothing, but I want something."

So Grethel gave Hans a needle. And then he said,

"Good-bye, Grethel," and she said, "Good-bye, Hans."

Hans carried the needle away with him, and stuck it in a hay cart that was going along, and he followed it home.

"Good evening, Mother."

"Good evening, Hans. Where have you been?"

"To Grethel's, Mother."

"What did you take her?"

"I took nothing, but I brought away something."

"What did Grethel give you?"

"A needle, mother."

"What did you do with it, Hans?"

"Stuck it in the hay cart."

"That was very stupid of you, Hans. You should have stuck it in your sleeve."

"All right, Mother! I'll do better next time."

When next time came, Hans's mother said,

"Where are you going, Hans?"

"To Grethel's, Mother."

"Manage well, Hans."

"All right! Good-bye, Mother."

"Good-bye, Hans."

Then Hans came to Grethel.

"Good morning, Grethel."

"Good morning, Hans. What have you brought me today?"

"I've brought nothing, but I want something."

So Grethel gave Hans a knife, and then he said, "Good-bye, Grethel," and she said, "Good-bye, Hans."

Hans took the knife away with him, and stuck it in his sleeve, and went home.

"Good evening, Mother."

"Good evening, Hans. Where have you been?"

"To Grethel's."

"What did you take her?"

"I took nothing, but I brought away something."

"What did Grethel give you, Hans?"

"A knife, Mother."

"What did you do with it, Hans?"

"Stuck it in my sleeve, Mother."

"That was very stupid of you, Hans. You should have put it in your pocket."

"All right, Mother! I'll do better next time."

When next time came, Hans's mother said,

"Where to, Hans?"

"To Grethel's, Mother."

"Manage well, Hans."

"All right! Good-bye, Mother."

"Good-bye, Hans."

So Hans came to Grethel's. "Good morning, Grethel."

"Good morning, Hans. What have you brought me to-day?"

"I've brought nothing, but I want to take away something."

So Grethel gave Hans a young goat. Then he said,

"Good-bye, Grethel," and she said, "Good-bye, Hans."

So Hans carried off the goat, and tied its legs together, and put it in his pocket, and by the time he got home it was suffocated.

"Good evening, Mother."

"Good evening, Hans. Where have you been?"

"To Grethel's, Mother."

"What did you take her, Hans?"

"I took nothing, but I brought away something."

"What did Grethel give you, Hans?"

"A goat, mother."

"What did you do with it, Hans?"

"Put it in my pocket, Mother."

"That was very stupid of you, Hans. You should have tied a cord round its neck, and led it home."

"All right, Mother! I'll do better next time."

Then when next time came,

"Where to, Hans?"

"To Grethel's, Mother."

"Manage well, Hans."

"All right! Good-bye, mother."

"Good-bye, Hans."

Then Hans came to Grethel's.

"Good morning, Grethel."

"Good morning, Hans. What have you brought me to-day?"

"I've brought nothing, but I want to take away something."

So Grethel gave Hans a piece of bacon. Then he said, "Good-bye, Grethel."

She said, "Good-bye, Hans."

Hans took the bacon, and tied a string round it, and dragged it after him on his way home, and the dogs came and ate it up, so that when he got home he had the string in his hand, and nothing at the other end of it.

"Good evening, Mother."

"Good evening, Hans. Where have you been?"

"To Grethel's, Mother."

"What did you take her, Hans?"

"I took her nothing, but I brought away something."

"What did Grethel give you, Hans?"

"A piece of bacon, Mother."

"What did you do with it, Hans?"

"I tied a piece of string to it, and led it home, but the dogs ate it, Mother."

"That was very stupid of you, Hans. You ought to have carried it on your head."

"All right! I'll do better next time, Mother."

When next time came,

"Where to, Hans?"

"To Grethel's, mother."

"Manage well, Hans."

"All right! Goodbye, Mother."

"Good-bye, Hans."

Then Hans came to Grethel's.

"Good morning, Grethel."

"Good morning, Hans. What have you brought me?"

"I have brought nothing, but I want to take away something."

So Grethel gave Hans a calf.

"Good-bye, Grethel."

"Good-bye, Hans."

Hans took the calf, and set it on his head, and carried it home, and the calf scratched his face.

"Good evening, Mother."

"Good evening, Hans. Where have you been?"

"To Grethel's, Mother."

"What did you take her?"

"I took nothing, but I brought away something."

"What did Grethel give you, Hans?"

"A calf, Mother."

"What did you do with the calf, Hans?"

"I carried it home on my head, but it scratched my face."

"That was very stupid of you, Hans. You ought to have led home the calf, and tied it to the manger."

"All right! I'll do better next time, Mother."

When next time came,

"Where to, Hans?"

"To Grethel's, Mother."

"Manage well, Hans."

"All right, Mother! Good-bye."

"Good-bye, Hans."

Then Hans came to Grethel's.

"Good morning, Grethel."

"Good morning, Hans. What have you brought me today?"

"I have brought nothing, but I want to take away something."

Then Grethel said to Hans,

"You shall take away me."

Then Hans took Grethel, and tied a rope round her neck, and led her home, and fastened her up to the manger, and went to his mother.

"Good evening, Mother."

"Good evening, Hans. Where have you been?"

"To Grethel's, Mother."

"What did you take her, Hans?"

"Nothing, Mother."

"What did Grethel give you, Hans?"

"Nothing but herself, Mother."

"Where have you left Grethel, Hans?"

"I led her home with a rope, and tied her up to the manger to eat hay, Mother."

"That was very stupid of you, Hans. You should have cast sheep's eyes at her."

"All right, Mother! I'll do better next time."

Then Hans went into the stable, and taking all the eyes out of the sheep, he threw them in Grethel's face. Then Grethel was angry, and getting loose, she ran away and became the bride of another.

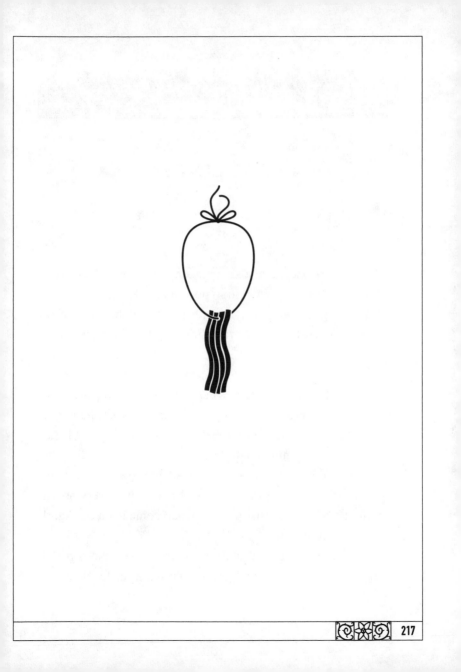

THE ELVES

There was once a shoemaker, who, through no fault of his own, became so poor that at last he had nothing left but just enough leather to make one pair of shoes. He cut out the shoes at night, so as to set to work upon them next morning. And as he had a good conscience, he laid himself quietly down in his bed, committed himself to heaven, and fell asleep. In the morning, after he had said his prayers, and was going to get to work, he found the pair of shoes made and finished, and standing on his table. He was very much astonished, and could not tell what to think, and he took the shoes in his hand to examine them more nearly. And they were so well made that every stitch was in its right place, just as if they had come from the hand of a master workman.

Soon after a purchaser entered, and as the shoes fitted him very well, he gave more than the usual price for them, so that the shoemaker had enough money to buy leather for two more pairs of shoes. He cut them out at night, and intended to set to work the next morning with fresh spirit. But that was not to be, for when he got up they were already finished, and a customer even was not lacking, who gave him so much money that he was able to buy leather enough for four new pairs. Early next morning he found the four pairs also finished, and so it always happened. Whatever he cut out in the evening was worked up by the morning, so that he was soon in the way of making a good living, and in the end became very well to do.

One night, not long before Christmas, when the shoemaker had finished cutting out, and before he went to bed, he said to his wife,

"How would it be if we were to sit up tonight and see who it is that does us this service?"

His wife agreed, and set a light to burn. Then they both hid in a corner of the room, behind some coats that were hanging up, and then they began to watch. As soon as it was midnight they saw come in two naked little men, who seated themselves before the shoemaker's table, and took up the work that was already prepared, and began to stitch, to pierce, and to hammer so cleverly and quickly with their little fingers that the shoemaker's eyes could scarcely follow them, so full of wonder was he. And they never left off until everything was finished and was standing ready on the table, and then they jumped up and ran off.

The next morning the shoemaker's wife said to her husband, "Those little men have made us rich, and we ought to show ourselves grateful. With all their running about, and having nothing to cover them, they must be very cold. I'll tell you what. I will make little shirts, coats, waistcoats, and breeches for them, and knit each of them a pair of stockings, and you shall make each of them a pair of shoes."

The husband consented willingly, and at night, when everything was finished, they laid the gifts together on the table, instead of the shoe work, and placed themselves so that they could observe how the little men would behave. When midnight came, they rushed in, ready to set to work, but when they found, instead of the pieces of prepared leather, the neat little garments put ready for them, they stood a moment in surprise, and then they testified the greatest delight. With the greatest swiftness they took up the pretty garments and slipped them on, singing,

"What spruce and dandy boys are we!
No longer cobblers we will be."

Then they hopped and danced about, jumping over the chairs and tables, and at last they danced out at the door.

From that time they were never seen again. But it always went well with the shoemaker as long as he lived, and whatever he took in hand prospered.

There was once a poor servant maid, who was very cleanly and industrious. She swept down the house every day, and put the sweepings on a great heap by the door. One morning, before she began her work, she found a letter, and as she could not read, she laid her broom in the corner, and took the letter to her master and mistress, to see what it was about. And it was an invitation from the elves, who wished the maid to come and stand godmother to one of their children. The maid did not know what to do. And as she was told that no one ought to refuse the elves anything, she made up her mind to go. So there came three little elves, who conducted her into the middle of a high mountain, where the little people lived. Here everything was of a very small size, but more fine and elegant than can be told. The mother of the child lay in a bed made of ebony, studded with pearls, the counterpane was embroidered with gold, the cradle was of ivory, and the bathing tub of gold. So the maid stood godmother, and was then for going home, but the elves begged her to stay at least three more days with them. And so she consented, and spent the time in mirth and jollity, and the elves seemed very fond of her. At last, when she was ready to go away, they filled her pockets full of gold, and led her back again out of the mountain. When she got back to the house, she was going to begin working again, and took her broom in her hand. It was still standing in the corner where she had left it, and began to sweep. Then came up some strangers and asked her who she was, and what she was doing. And she found that instead of three days, she had been seven years with the elves in the mountain, and that during that time her master and mistress had died.

{III}

The elves once took a child away from its mother, and left in its place a changeling with a big head and staring eyes, who did nothing but eat and drink. The mother in her trouble went to her neighbors and asked their advice. The neighbors told her to take the changeling into the kitchen and put it near the hearth, and then to make up the fire, and boil water in two eggshells. That would make the changeling laugh, and if he laughed, it would be all over with him. So the woman did as her neighbors advised. And when she set the eggshells of water on the fire, the changeling said,

> "Though old I be
> As forest tree,
> Cooking in an eggshell never did I see!"

and began to laugh. And directly there came in a crowd of elves bringing in the right child. And they laid it near the hearth, and carried the changeling away with them.

SNOW WHITE

t was the middle of winter, and the snowflakes were falling like feathers from the sky, and a Queen sat at her window working, and her embroidery frame was of ebony. And as she worked, gazing at times out on the snow, she pricked her finger, and there fell from it three drops of blood on the snow. And when she saw how bright and red it looked, she said to herself, "Oh that I had a child as white as snow, as red as blood, and as black as the wood of the embroidery frame!"

Not very long after she had a daughter, with a skin as white as snow, lips as red as blood, and hair as black as ebony, and she was named Snow White. And when she was born the Queen died.

After a year had gone by the King took another wife, a beautiful woman, but proud and overbearing, and she could not bear to be surpassed in beauty by any one. She had a magic looking-glass, and she used to stand before it, and look in it, and say,

"Looking-glass upon the wall,
Who is fairest of us all?"

And the looking-glass would answer,

"You are fairest of them all."

And she was contented, for she knew that the looking-glass spoke the truth.

Now, Snow White was growing prettier and prettier, and when she was seven years old she was as beautiful as day, far more so than the Queen herself. So one day when the Queen went to her mirror and said,

"Looking-glass upon the wall,
Who is fairest of us all?"

It answered,

"Queen, you are full fair, 'tis true,
But Snow White fairer is than you."

This gave the Queen a great shock, and she became yellow and green with envy, and from that hour her heart turned against Snow White, and she hated her. And envy and pride like ill weeds grew in her heart higher every day, until she had no peace day or night. At last she sent for a huntsman, and said,

"Take the child out into the woods, so that I may set eyes on her no more. You must put her to death, and bring me her heart for a token."

The huntsman consented, and led her away. But when he drew his cutlass to pierce Snow White's innocent heart, she began to weep, and to say,

"Oh, dear huntsman, do not take my life. I will go away into the wild wood, and never come home again."

And as she was so lovely the huntsman had pity on her, and said,

"Away with you then, poor child," for he thought the wild animals would be sure to devour her, and it was as if a stone had been rolled away from his heart when he spared to put her to death. Just at that moment a young wild boar came running by, so he caught and killed it, and taking out its heart, he brought it to the Queen for a token. And it was salted and cooked, and the wicked woman ate it up, thinking that there was an end of Snow White.

Now, when the poor child found herself quite alone in the wild woods, she felt full of terror, even of the very leaves on the trees, and she did not know what to do for fright. Then she began to run over the sharp stones and through the thorn bushes, and the wild beasts after her, but they did her no harm. She ran as long as her feet would carry her. And when the evening drew near she came to a little house, and she went inside to rest. Everything there was very small, but as pretty and clean as possible. There stood the little table ready laid, and covered with a white cloth, and seven little plates, and seven knives and forks, and drinking cups. By the wall stood seven little beds, side by side, covered with clean white quilts. Snow White, being very hungry and thirsty, ate from each plate a little porridge and bread, and drank out of each little cup a drop of wine, so as not to finish up one portion alone. After that she felt so tired that she lay down on one of the beds, but it did not seem to suit her. One was too long, another too short, but at last the seventh was quite right. And so she lay down upon it, committed herself to heaven, and fell asleep.

When it was quite dark, the masters of the house came home. They were seven dwarfs, whose occupation was to dig underground among the mountains. When they had lighted their seven candles, and it was quite light in the little house, they saw that someone must have been in, as everything was not in the same order in which they left it. The first said,

"Who has been sitting in my little chair?"

The second said,

"Who has been eating from my little plate?"

The third said,

"Who has been taking my little loaf?"

The fourth said,

"Who has been tasting my porridge?"

The fifth said,

"Who has been using my little fork?"

The sixth said,

"Who has been cutting with my little knife?"

The seventh said,

"Who has been drinking from my little cup?"

Then the first one, looking round, saw a hollow in his bed, and cried,

"Who has been lying on my bed?"

And the others came running, and cried,

"Someone has been on our beds too!"

But when the seventh looked at his bed, he saw little Snow White lying there asleep. Then he told the others, who came running up, crying out in their astonishment, and holding up their seven little candles to throw a light upon Snow White.

"O goodness! O gracious!" cried they. "What beautiful child is this?" and were so full of joy to see her that they did not wake her, but let her sleep on. And the seventh dwarf slept with his comrades, an hour at a time with each, until the night had passed.

When it was morning, and Snow White awoke and saw the seven dwarfs, she was very frightened. But they seemed quite friendly, and asked her what her name was, and she told them. And then they asked how she came to be in their house.

And she related to them how her stepmother had wished her to be put to death, and how the huntsman had spared her life, and how she had run the whole day long, until at last she had found their little house. Then the dwarfs said,

"If you will keep our house for us, and cook, and wash, and make the beds, and sew and knit, and keep everything tidy and clean, you may stay with us, and you shall lack nothing."

"With all my heart," said Snow White. And so she stayed, and kept the house in good order. In the morning the dwarfs went to the mountain to dig for gold. In the evening they came home, and their supper had to be ready for them. All day long the maiden was left alone, and the good little dwarfs warned her, saying,

"Beware of your stepmother. She will soon know you are here. Let no one into the house."

Now the Queen, having eaten Snow White's heart, as she supposed, felt quite sure that now she was the first and fairest, and so she came to her mirror, and said,

"Looking-glass upon the wall,
Who is fairest of us all?"

And the glass answered,

"Queen, thou art of beauty rare,
But Snow White living in the glen

With the seven little men
Is a thousand times more fair."

Then she was very angry, for the glass always spoke the truth, and she knew that the huntsman must have deceived her, and that Snow White must still be living. And she thought and thought how she could manage to make an end of her, for as long as she was not the fairest in the land, envy left her no rest. At last she thought of a plan. She painted her face and dressed herself like an old peddler woman, so that no one would have known her. In this disguise she went across the seven mountains, until she came to the house of the seven little dwarfs, and she knocked at the door and cried,

"Fine wares to sell! Fine wares to sell!"

Snow White peeped out of the window and cried,

"Good day, good woman, what have you to sell?"

"Good wares, fine wares," answered she. "Laces of all colors," and she held up a piece that was woven of variegated silk.

"I need not be afraid of letting in this good woman," thought Snow White, and she unbarred the door and bought the pretty lace.

"What a figure you are, child!" said the old woman. "Come and let me lace you properly for once."

Snow White, suspecting nothing, stood up before her, and let her lace her with the new lace. But the old woman laced so quick and tight that it took Snow White's breath away, and she fell down as dead.

"Now you have done with being the fairest," said the old woman as she hastened away.

Not long after that, towards evening, the seven dwarfs came home, and were terrified to see their dear Snow White lying on the ground, without life or motion. They raised her up, and when they saw how tightly she was laced they cut the lace in two. Then she began to draw breath, and little by little she returned to life. When the dwarfs heard what had happened they said,

"The old peddler woman was no other than the wicked Queen. You must beware of letting anyone in when we are not here!"

And when the wicked woman got home she went to her glass and said,

"Looking-glass against the wall,
Who is fairest of us all?"

And it answered as before,

"Queen, thou art of beauty rare,
But Snow White living in the glen
With the seven little men
Is a thousand times more fair."

When she heard that she was so struck with surprise that all the blood left her heart, for she knew that Snow White must still be living.

"But now," said she, "I will think of something that will be her ruin." And by witchcraft she made a poisoned comb. Then she dressed herself up to look like another different sort of old woman. So she went across the seven mountains and came to the house of the seven dwarfs, and knocked at the door and cried,

"Good wares to sell! Good wares to sell!"

Snow White looked out and said,

"Go away, I must not let anybody in."

"But you are not forbidden to look," said the old woman, taking out the poisoned comb and holding it up. It pleased the poor child so much that she was tempted to open the door. And when the bargain was made the old woman said,

"Now, for once your hair shall be properly combed."

Poor Snow White, thinking no harm, let the old woman do as she would, but no sooner was the comb put in her hair than the poison began to work, and the poor girl fell down senseless.

"Now, you paragon of beauty," said the wicked woman, "this is the end of you," and went off. By good luck it was now near evening, and the seven little dwarfs came home. When they saw Snow White lying on the ground as dead, they thought directly that it was the stepmother's doing, and looked about, found the poisoned comb, and no sooner had they drawn it out of her hair than Snow White came to herself, and related all that had passed. Then they warned her once more to be on her guard, and never again to let anyone in at the door.

And the Queen went home and stood before the looking-glass and said,

"Looking-glass against the wall,
Who is fairest of us all?"

And the looking glass answered as before,

"Queen, thou art of beauty rare,
But Snow White living in the glen
With the seven little men
Is a thousand times more fair."

When she heard the looking-glass speak thus she trembled and shook with anger.

"Snow White shall die," cried she. "Though it should cost me my own life!" And then she went to a secret lonely chamber, where no one was likely to come, and there she made a poisonous apple. It was beautiful to look upon, being white with red cheeks, so that anyone who should see it must long for it, but whoever ate even a little bit of it must die. When the apple was ready she painted her face and clothed herself like a peasant woman, and went across the seven mountains to where the seven dwarfs lived. And when she knocked at the door Snow White put her head out of the window and said,

"I dare not let anybody in. The seven dwarfs told me not."

"All right," answered the woman. "I can easily get rid of my apples elsewhere. There, I will give you one."

"No," answered Snow White. "I dare not take anything."

"Are you afraid of poison?" said the woman. "Look here, I will cut the apple in two pieces. You shall have the red side, I will have the white one."

For the apple was so cunningly made, that all the poison was in the rosy half of it. Snow White longed for the beautiful apple, and as she saw the peasant woman eating a piece of it she could no longer refrain, but stretched out her hand and took the poisoned half. But no sooner had she taken a morsel of it into her mouth than she fell to the earth as dead. And the Queen, casting on her a terrible glance, laughed aloud and cried,

"As white as snow, as red as blood, as black as ebony! This time the dwarfs will not be able to bring you to life again."

And when she went home and asked the looking-glass,

"Looking-glass against the wall,
Who is fairest of us all?"

At last it answered,

"You are the fairest now of all."

Then her envious heart had peace, as much as an envious heart can have.

The dwarfs, when they came home in the evening, found Snow White lying on the ground, and there came no breath out of her mouth, and she was dead. They lifted her up, sought if anything poisonous was to be found, cut her laces, combed her hair, washed her with water and wine, but all was of no avail, the poor child was dead, and remained dead. Then they laid her on a bier, and sat all seven of them round it, and wept and lamented three whole days. And then they would have buried her, but that she looked still as if she were living, with her beautiful blooming cheeks. So they said,

"We cannot hide her away in the black ground." And they had made a coffin of clear glass, so as to be looked into from all sides, and they laid her in it, and wrote in golden letters upon it her name, and that she was a King's daughter. Then they set the coffin out upon the mountain, and one of them always remained by it to watch. And the birds came too, and mourned for Snow White, first an owl, then a raven, and lastly, a dove.

Now, for a long while Snow White lay in the coffin and never changed, but looked as if she were asleep, for she was still as white as snow, as red as blood, and her hair was as black as ebony. It happened, however, that one day a King's son rode through the wood and up to the dwarfs' house, which was near it. He saw on the mountain the coffin, and beautiful Snow White within it, and he read what was written in golden letters upon it. Then he said to the dwarfs,

"Let me have the coffin, and I will give you whatever you like to ask for it."

But the dwarfs told him that they could not part with it for all the gold in the world. But he said,

"I beseech you to give it me, for I cannot live without looking upon Snow White. If you consent I will bring you to great honor, and care for you as if you were my brethren."

When he so spoke the good little dwarfs had pity upon him and gave him the coffin, and the King's son called his servants and bid them carry it away on their shoulders. Now it happened that as they were going along they stumbled over a bush, and with the shaking the bit of poisoned apple flew out of her throat. It was not long before she opened her eyes, threw up the cover of the coffin, and sat up, alive and well.

"Oh dear! Where am I?" cried she. The King's son answered, full of joy, "You are near me," and, relating all that had happened, he said,

"I would rather have you than anything in the world. Come with me to my father's castle and you shall be my bride."

And Snow White was kind, and went with him, and their wedding was held with pomp and great splendor.

But Snow White's wicked stepmother was also bidden

to the feast, and when she had dressed herself in beautiful clothes she went to her looking glass and said,

> "Looking-glass upon the wall,
> Who is fairest of us all?"

The looking-glass answered,

> "O Queen, although you are of beauty rare,
> The young bride is a thousand times more fair."

Then she railed and cursed, and was beside herself with disappointment and anger. First she thought she would not go to the wedding. But then she felt she should have no peace until she went and saw the bride. And when she saw her she knew her for Snow White, and could not stir from the place for anger and terror. For they had ready red-hot iron shoes, in which she had to dance until she fell down dead.

THE SIX SWANS

Once on a time a King was hunting in a great wood, and he pursued a wild animal so eagerly that none of his people could follow him. When evening came he stood still, and looking round him he found that he had lost his way. And seeking a path, he found none. Then all at once he saw an old woman with a nodding head coming up to him. And it was a witch.

"My good woman," said he, "can you show me the way out of the wood?"

"Oh yes, my lord King," answered she. "Certainly I can. But I must make a condition, and if you do not fulfill it, you will never get out of the wood again, but die there of hunger."

"What is the condition?" asked the King.

"I have a daughter," said the old woman, "who is as fair as any in the world, and if you will take her for your bride, and make her Queen, I will show you the way out of the wood."

The King consented, because of the difficulty he was in,

and the old woman led him into her little house, and there her daughter was sitting by the fire.

She received the King just as if she had been expecting him, and though he saw that she was very beautiful, she did not please him, and he could not look at her without an inward shudder. Nevertheless, he took the maiden before him on his horse, and the old woman showed him the way, and soon he was in his royal castle again, where the wedding was held.

The King had been married before, and his first wife had left seven children, six boys and one girl, whom he loved better than all the world, and as he was afraid the stepmother might not behave well to them, and perhaps would do them some mischief, he took them to a lonely castle standing in the middle of a wood. There they remained hidden, for the road to it was so hard to find that the King himself could not have found it, had it not been for a ball of yarn, possessing wonderful properties, that a wise woman had given him. When he threw it down before him, it unrolled itself and showed him the way. And the King went so often to see his dear children, that the Queen was displeased at his absence. And she became curious and wanted to know what he went out into the wood for so often alone. She bribed his servants with much money, and they showed her the secret, and told her of the clue of yarn, which alone could point out the way. Then she gave herself no rest until she had found out where the King kept the ball, and then she made some little white silk shirts, and sewed a charm in each, as she had learned witchcraft of her mother. And once when the King had ridden to the hunt, she took the little shirts and went into the wood, and the clue of yarn showed her the way. The children, seeing someone in the distance, thought it was their dear father coming to see them, and came jumping for joy to meet him. Then the wicked Queen threw over each one of the little shirts, and as soon as the shirts touched their bodies, they were changed into swans, and flew away through the wood. So the Queen went home very pleased to think she had got rid of her step-children. But the maiden had not run out with her brothers, and so the Queen knew nothing about her. The next day the King went to see his children, but he found nobody but his daughter.

"Where are thy brothers?" asked the King.

"Ah, dear father," answered she. "They are gone away and have left me behind," and then she told him how she had seen from her window her brothers in the guise of swans fly away through the wood, and she showed him the feathers which they had let fall in the courtyard, and which she had picked up. The King was grieved, but he never dreamt that it was the Queen who had done this wicked deed, and as he feared lest the maiden also should be stolen away from him, he wished to take her away with him. But she was afraid of the stepmother, and begged the King to let her remain one more night in the castle in the wood.

Then she said to herself,

"I must stay here no longer, but go and seek for my brothers."

And when the night came, she fled away and went straight into the wood. She went on all that night and the next day, until she could go no longer for weariness. At last she saw a rude hut, and she went in and found a room with six little beds in it. She did not dare to lie down in one, but she crept under one and lay on the hard boards and wished for night. When it was near the time of sun setting she heard a rustling sound, and saw six swans come flying in at the window. They alighted on the ground, and blew at one another until they had blown all their feathers off, and then they stripped off their swan skin as if it had been a shirt. And the maiden looked at them and knew them for her brothers, and was very glad, and crept from under the bed. The brothers were not less glad when their sister appeared, but their joy did not last long.

"You must not stay here," said they to her. "This is a robbers' haunt, and if they were to come and find you here, they would kill you."

"And cannot you defend me?" asked the little sister.

"No," answered they, "for we can only get rid of our swan skins and keep our human shape every evening for a quarter of an hour, but after that we must be changed again into swans."

Their sister wept at hearing this, and said,

"Can nothing be done to set you free?"

"Oh no," answered they. "The work would be too hard for you. For six whole years you would be obliged never to speak or laugh, and make during that time six little shirts out of aster flowers. If you were to let fall a single word before the work was ended, all would be of no good."

And just as the brothers had finished telling her this, the quarter of an hour came to an end, and they changed into swans and flew out of the window.

But the maiden made up her mind to set her brothers free, even though it should cost her her life. She left the hut, and going into the middle of the wood, she climbed a tree, and there passed the night. The next morning she set to work and gathered asters and began sewing them together. As for speaking, there was no one to speak to, and as for laughing, she had no mind to it. So she sat on and looked at nothing but her work. When she had been going on like this for a long time, it happened that the King of that country went hunting in the wood, and some of his huntsmen came up to the tree in which the maiden sat. They called out to her, saying, "Who art thou?" But she gave no answer. "Come down," cried they. "We will do thee no harm." But she only shook her head. And when they tormented her further with questions she threw down to them her gold necklace, hoping they would be content with that. But they would not leave off, so she threw down to them her girdle, and when that was no good, her garters, and one after another everything she had on and could possibly spare, until she had nothing left but her smock. But all was no good, the huntsmen would not be put off any longer, and they climbed the tree, carried the maiden off, and brought her to the King. The King asked, "Who art thou? What wert thou doing in the tree?" But she answered nothing. He spoke to her in all the languages he knew, but she remained dumb. But, being very beautiful, the King inclined to her, and he felt a great love rise up in his heart towards her. And casting his mantle round her, he put her before him on his horse and brought her to his castle. Then he caused rich clothing to be put upon her, and her beauty shone as bright as the morning, but no word would she utter. He seated her by his side at table, and her modesty and gentle disposition so pleased him, that he said,

"This maiden I choose for wife, and no other in all the world," and accordingly after a few days they were married.

But the King had a wicked mother, who was displeased with the marriage, and spoke ill of the young Queen.

"Who knows where the maid can have come from?" said she. "And not able to speak a word! She is not worthy of a King!"

After a year had passed, and the Queen brought her first child into the world, the old woman carried it away, and marked the Queen's mouth with blood as she lay sleeping. Then she went to the King and declared that his wife was an eater of human flesh. The King would not believe such a thing, and ordered that no one should do her any harm. And the Queen went on quietly sewing the shirts and caring for nothing else. The next time that a fine boy was born, the wicked stepmother used the same deceit, but the King would give no credence to her words, for he said,

"She is too tender and good to do any such thing, and if she were only not dumb, and could justify herself, then her innocence would be as clear as day."

When for the third time the old woman stole away the newborn child and accused the Queen, who was unable to say a word in her defense, the King could do no other but give her up to justice, and she was sentenced to suffer death by fire.

The day on which her sentence was to be carried out was the very last one of the sixth year of the years during which she had neither spoken nor laughed, to free her dear brothers from the evil spell. The six shirts were ready, all except one which wanted the left sleeve. And when she was led to the pile of wood, she carried the six shirts on her arm, and when she mounted the pile and the fire was about to be kindled, all at once she cried out aloud, for there were six swans coming flying through the air. And she saw that her deliverance was near, and her heart beat for joy. The swans came close up to her with rushing wings, and stooped round her, so that she could throw the shirts over them. And when that had been done the swan skins fell off them, and her brothers stood before her in their own bodies quite safe and sound. But as one shirt wanted the left sleeve, so the youngest brother had a swan's wing instead of a left arm. They embraced and kissed each other, and the Queen went up to the King, who looked on full of astonishment, and began to speak to him and to say,

"Dearest husband, now I may dare to speak and tell you that I am innocent, and have been falsely accused." And she related to him the treachery of the stepmother, who had taken away the three children and hidden them. And she was reconciled to the King with great joy, and the wicked stepmother was bound to the stake on the pile of wood and burnt to ashes.

And the King and Queen lived many years with their six brothers in peace and joy.

CLEVER GRETHEL

There was once a cook called Grethel, who wore shoes with red heels, and when she went out in them she gave herself great airs, and thought herself very fine indeed. When she came home again, she would take a drink of wine to refresh herself, and as that gave her an appetite, she would take some of the best of whatever she was cooking, until she had had enough. "For," said she, "a cook must know how things taste."

Now it happened that one day her master said to her,

"Grethel, I expect a guest this evening. You must make ready a pair of fowls."

"Certainly, sir, I will," answered Grethel. So she killed the fowls, cleaned them, and plucked them, and put them on the spit, and then, as evening drew near, placed them before the fire to roast. And they began to be brown, and were nearly done, but the guest had not come.

"If he does not make haste," cried Grethel to her master, "I must take them away from the fire. It's a pity and a shame not to eat them now, just when they are done to a turn." And the master said he would run himself and fetch the guest. As soon as he had turned his back, Grethel took the fowls from before the fire.

"Standing so long before the fire," said she, "makes one hot and thirsty, and who knows when they will come! In the meanwhile I will go to the cellar and have a drink." So down she ran, took up a mug, and saying, "Here's to me!" took a good draught. "One good drink deserves another," she said, "and it should not be cut short." So she took another hearty draught. Then she went and put the fowls down to the fire again, and, basting them with butter, she turned the spit briskly round. And now they began to smell so good that Grethel, saying, "I must find out whether they really are all right," licked her fingers. Then she cried, "Well, I never! The fowls are good. It's a sin and a shame that no one is here to eat them!"

So she ran to the window to see if her master and his guest were coming, but as she could see nobody she went back to her fowls. "Why, one of the wings is burning!" she cried presently. "I had better eat it and get it out of the way." So she cut it off and ate it up, and it tasted good, and then she thought,

"I had better cut off the other too, in case the master should miss anything." And when both wings had been disposed of she went and looked for the master, but still he did not come.

"Who knows," said she, "whether they are coming or not? They may have put up at an inn." And after a pause she said again, "Come, I may as well make myself happy, and first I will make sure of a good drink and then of a good meal, and when all is done I shall be easy. The gifts of the gods are not to be despised." So first she ran down into the cellar and had a famous drink, and ate up one of the fowls with great relish. And when that was done, and still the master did not come, Grethel eyed the other fowl, saying, "What one is the other must be, the two belong to each other, it is only fair that they should be both treated alike. Perhaps, when I have had another drink, I shall be able to manage it." So she took another hearty drink, and then the second fowl went the way of the first.

Just as she was in the middle of it the master came back. "Make haste, Grethel," cried he. "The guest is coming directly!" "Very well, master," she answered, "it will soon be ready." The master went to see that the table was properly laid, and, taking the great carving knife with which he meant to carve the fowls, he sharpened it upon the step. Presently came the guest, knocking very genteelly and softly at the front door. Grethel ran and looked to see who it was, and when she caught sight of the guest she put her finger on her lip saying, "Hush! Make the best haste you can out of this, for if my master catches you, it will be bad for you. He asked you to come to supper, but he really means to cut off your ears! Just listen how he is sharpening his knife!"

The guest, hearing the noise of the sharpening, made off as fast as he could go. And Grethel ran screaming to her master. "A pretty guest you have asked to the house!" cried she.

"How so, Grethel? What do you mean?" asked he.

"What indeed!" said she. "Why, he has gone and run away with my pair of fowls that I had just dished up."

"That's a pretty sort of conduct!" said the master, feeling very sorry about the fowls. "He might at least have left me one, that I might have had something to eat." And he called out to him to stop, but the guest made as if he did not hear him. Then he ran after him, the knife still in his hand, crying out "Only one! only one!" meaning that the guest should let him have one of the fowls and not take both, but the guest thought he meant to have only one of his ears, and he ran so much the faster that he might get home with both of them safe.

THE FROG PRINCE

I n the old times, when it was still of some use to wish for the thing one wanted, there lived a King whose daughters were all handsome, but the youngest was so beautiful that the sun himself, who has seen so much, wondered each time he shone over her because of her beauty. Near the royal castle there was a great dark wood, and in the wood under an old linden tree was a well. And when the day was hot, the King's daughter used to go forth into the wood and sit by the brink of the cool well, and if the time seemed long, she would take out a golden ball, and throw it up and catch it again, and this was her favorite pastime.

Now it happened one day that the golden ball, instead of falling back into the maiden's little hand which had sent it aloft, dropped to the ground near the edge of the well and rolled in. The King's daughter followed it with her eyes as it sank, but the well was deep, so deep that the bottom could not be seen. Then she began to weep, and she wept and wept as if she could never be comforted. And in the midst of her weeping she heard a voice saying to her,

"What ails thee, King's daughter? Thy tears would melt a heart of stone."

And when she looked to see where the voice came from, there was nothing but a frog stretching his thick ugly head out of the water.

"Oh, is it you, old waddler?" said she. "I weep because my golden ball has fallen into the well."

"Never mind, do not weep," answered the frog. "I can help you. But what will you give me if I fetch up your ball again?"

"Whatever you like, dear frog," said she. "Any of my clothes, my pearls and jewels, or even the golden crown that I wear."

"Thy clothes, thy pearls and jewels, and thy golden crown are not for me," answered the frog. "But if thou wouldst love me, and have me for thy companion and play-fellow, and let me sit by thee at table, and eat from thy plate, and drink from thy cup, and sleep in thy little bed, if thou wouldst promise all this, then would I dive below the water and fetch thee thy golden ball again."

"Oh yes," she answered. "I will promise it all, whatever you want, if you will only get me my ball again."

But she thought to herself, "What nonsense he talks! As if he could do anything but sit in the water and croak with the other frogs, or could possibly be any one's companion."

But the frog, as soon as he heard her promise, drew his head under the water and sank down out of sight, but after a while he came to the surface again with the ball in his mouth, and he threw it on the grass.

The King's daughter was overjoyed to see her pretty plaything again, and she caught it up and ran off with it.

"Stop, stop!" cried the frog. "Take me up too. I cannot run as fast as you!"

But it was of no use, for croak, croak after her as he might, she would not listen to him, but made haste home, and very soon forgot all about the poor frog, who had to betake himself to his well again.

The next day, when the King's daughter was sitting at table with the King and all the court, and eating from her golden plate, there came something pitter-patter up the marble stairs, and then there came a knocking at the door, and a voice crying, "Youngest King's daughter, let me in!"

And she got up and ran to see who it could be, but when she opened the door, there was the frog sitting outside. Then she shut the door hastily and went back to her seat, feeling very uneasy. The King noticed how quickly her heart was beating, and said,

"My child, what are you afraid of? Is there a giant standing at the door ready to carry you away?"

"Oh no," answered she. "No giant, but a horrid frog."

"And what does the frog want?" asked the King.

"O dear Father," answered she. "When I was sitting by the well yesterday, and playing with my golden ball, it fell into the water, and while I was crying for the loss of it, the frog came and got it again for me on condition I would let him be my companion, but I never thought that he could leave the water and come after me. But now there he is outside the door and he wants to come in to me."

And then they all heard him knocking the second time and crying,

"Youngest King's daughter,
Open to me!
By the well water
What promised you me?
Youngest King's daughter
Now open to me!"

"That which thou hast promised must thou perform," said the King. "So go now and let him in."

So she went and opened the door, and the frog hopped in, following at her heels, till she reached her chair. Then he stopped and cried,

"Lift me up to sit by you."

But she delayed doing so until the King ordered her. When once the frog was on the chair, he wanted to get on the table, and there he sat and said,

"Now push your golden plate a little nearer, so that we may eat together."

And so she did, but everybody might see how unwilling she was, and the frog feasted heartily, but every morsel seemed to stick in her throat.

"I have had enough now," said the frog at last. "And as I am tired, you must carry me to your room, and make ready your silken bed, and we will lie down and go to sleep."

Then the King's daughter began to weep, and was afraid of the cold frog, that nothing would satisfy him but he must sleep in her pretty clean bed. Now the King grew angry with her, saying,

"That which thou hast promised in thy time of necessity, must thou now perform."

So she picked up the frog with her finger and thumb, carried him upstairs, and put him in a corner, and when she had lain down to sleep, he came creeping up, saying, "I am tired and want sleep as much as you. Take me up, or I will tell your father."

Then she felt beside herself with rage, and picking him up, she threw him with all her strength against the wall, crying,

"Now will you be quiet, you horrid frog!"

But as he fell, he ceased to be a frog, and became all at once a prince with beautiful kind eyes. And it came to pass that, with her father's consent, they became bride and bridegroom. And he told her how a wicked witch had bound him by her spells, and how no one but she alone could have released him, and that they two would go together to his father's kingdom. And there came to the door a carriage drawn by eight white horses, with white plumes on their heads, and with golden harness, and behind the carriage was standing faithful Henry, the servant of the young prince. Now, faithful Henry had suffered such care and pain when his master was turned into a frog, that he had been obliged to wear three iron bands over his heart, to keep it from breaking with trouble and anxiety. When the carriage started to take the prince to his kingdom, and faithful Henry had helped them both in, he got up behind, and was full of joy at his master's deliverance. And when they had gone a part of the way, the prince heard a sound at the back of the carriage, as if something had broken, and he turned round and cried,

"Henry, the wheel must be breaking!" but Henry answered,

"The wheel does not break,
'Tis the band round my heart
That, to lessen its ache,
When I grieved for your sake,
I bound round my heart."

Again, and yet once again, there was the same sound, and the prince thought it must be the wheel breaking, but it was the breaking of the other bands from faithful Henry's heart, because it was now so relieved and happy.